Suddenly there was nothing ahead of *Venerable* but open water: the gap in the line. Something hummed through the air overhead and a second later the noise was repeated *fortissimo*, followed by the multiple reports of musketry from the ships on either side of the gap. The flagship's for'ard guns opened fire with a stunning concussion, initiating the running broadside that poured into the stern of the black-painted ship as they flew by. She was so close that he could have flung a stone into the great ragged hole that appeared as if by magic where two of the stern windows had been, and he could clearly see an officer pushing through the musketeers at the taffrail to level a pistol at him. The row of marines by the larboard rail in front of him fired their volley and officer and musketeers vanished from above the taffrail as if they had all been jerked back by strings. Then they were through the gap. . . .

*Also by Showell Styles and available from Sphere Books*

ADMIRAL OF ENGLAND

VINCEY JOE AT QUIBERON

# *Sea Road to Camperdown*

**SHOWELL STYLES**

SPHERE BOOKS LIMITED
30/32 Gray's Inn Road, London WC1X 8JL

First published in Great Britain by Faber & Faber Ltd 1968

Sphere Books edition published 1976

TRADE
MARK

Set in Linotype Times

Printed in Great Britain by
Hazell Watson & Viney Ltd
Aylesbury, Bucks

All the chief characters in this story actually existed. All the main events actually happened.

The letters and dispatches printed in italic are on historical record.

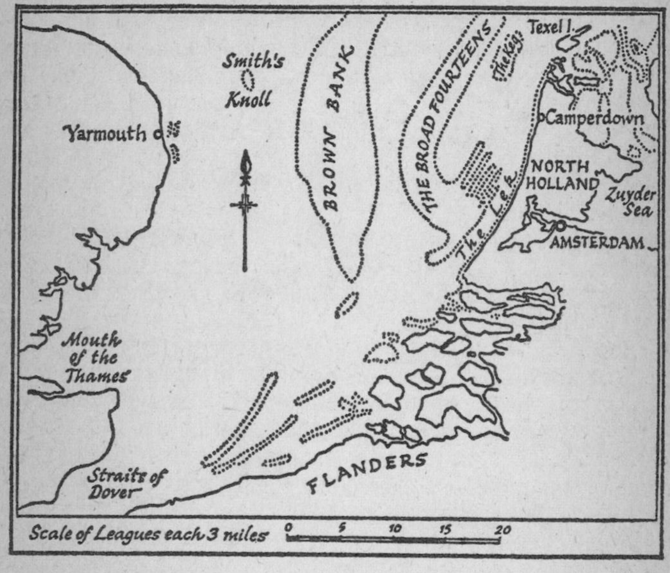


*North Sea and coast of Holland: based on the Chart by W. T. Davies, 1797*

# PROLOGUE

'Give us,' muttered the Prime Minister earnestly, 'give us the virtues which – which – damnation! – which adversity has never failed to evoke.'

He scrawled the words on the crumpled paper in front of him. The quill pen spluttered, speckling with ink the base of a half-empty wineglass. Across the red cloth of the table the Secretary for War sipped port and watched his friend with concern, his ruddy face creased in an unaccustomed frown. Billy can't stand this pace much longer, he was thinking; and if he cracks, who's to save the Government? For to Harry Dundas's political patriotism the saving of the Government – Pitt's Government – was the one hope of bringing England out from the shadow of this her darkest hour.

Pitt's quill had stopped spluttering. He was staring blankly at the wavering candle-flames on the triple-branch candelabrum that lit the table. In their yellowish light his features, gaunt and sharp-nosed, glistened faintly as with sweat though the parlour was cool in spite of the wood fire smouldering on the hearth. The sallow skin stretched over the cheekbones was unevenly blotched with faint colour.

'The virtues of adversity endured,' he murmured. 'No – of adversity endured and adversity resisted, of adversity encountered and adversity surmounted.' He bent again over his paper.

'Here's a wheen adversities, I'm thinking,' Dundas criticized.

The quill scratched on unheeding, then stopped. 'This is the great resource of the English character.' Pitt weighed the words before setting them down. 'By this we have preserved our existence—' The quill, with a final excruciating splutter, broke. 'Oh, pox on it!' cried Mr. Pitt angrily, flinging it down.

Dundas picked up the broken quill and dropped it into a basket full of crumpled sheets of paper that stood beside the table.

'Never mix ink and port, Billy,' he observed sagely.

'Stick to port when ye've supped and ye'll no' lose your temper. That's my advice. Forbye the speech can wait.'

The Prime Minister drained his glass. The Secretary had the bottle ready when he set it down, and splashed wine into it. Pitt emptied the glass in two gulps. The faint blotches on his cheeks took on a brighter hue.

'The Fleet sailed at noon, Harry,' he said feverishly. 'I must write or talk, for I dare not think about it.'

'No need to think.' Dundas poured him another bumper. 'They'll give a good account of themselves, never fear.'

'Account!' The other's voice was sharp. 'A good account is not enough. All hangs on this battle – all.'

'Aye, sir. If the Dutch will fight—'

'They *must* fight, Hal. And they must be beaten, destroyed. —Listen!'

The wind of the October night had risen in a passing gust, stirring the dark groves of Wimbledon with a sound like sea waves. There was a stir at the curtained windows and the candle-flames flickered nervously.

'North-easterly,' remarked Dundas, holding up his glass to admire the ruby glow. 'De Winter's ships will be out, dinna doubt that. And the Fleet will intercept 'em. Our lads will give the damned Batavian Republic the thrashing they've asked for.'

Pitt's glance at him held something like contempt. 'You are so confident, Hal? Have you given one thought to the ships, the men, we are sending against the finest fleet in Europe?' He leaned forward, a sombre gleam in his prominent eyes. 'The ships – twelve or fourteen of the line, all but a few scarce fit to put to sea. The men – four months ago in mutiny, ready for aught we know to mutiny again. Their admiral—'

'Now, now, Billy,' Dundas interrupted jovially. 'Ye'll no' have heard a single wee word against Adam Duncan.'

'Nor have I heard much to excite my confidence in Admiral Duncan.' Pitt's tone was cold. 'I believe him to be an honest, God-fearing gentleman. I know he owes his present command to the fact that he is your nephew by marriage.'

The Secretary chuckled. 'Aye – a nephew older than his uncle. I can give nevoy Adam eleven years, Billy.'

The Prime Minister stared at him incredulously. 'I had not thought – this is true, Hal? Duncan is sixty-six?'

'Sixty-six this past July. But I'll guarantee—'

'An old man,' Pitt muttered. 'Old ships, disaffected crews, and an old man in command. To this we have come. Duncan.' He frowned. 'Was he not to be retired with an Irish peerage this year?'

'Aye. But that's no' the measure of the man, Billy.' Dundas took off his wig, revealing a reddish poll in need of cropping, and wagged a serious finger. 'Adam's a proper seaman and knows his duty. He's well likit by the men. And he knows the Texel shoals as you and I know Whitehall. Drink up, man, and drown your fidgets.'

Pitt's bony hand grasped the glass automatically. As he tilted it the ruby wine glowed in the candlelight, dwindled, vanished. He set the glass down empty and glowered at it, widening and narrowing his eyes in a manner which Dundas, apprehensively, recognized as the preliminary to oratory. After a moment he spoke, his voice deepening into sonority as the words flowed from him.

'There was never a time in the history of Europe when Britain was nearer to her end. We stand alone. The Jacobin Republic has coerced the whole continent to her aid and stands poised to launch her hordes across the Channel, our sole defence. With what can we face them, if they land on English soil? With a bungling, incompetent rabble of uniformed jailbirds and tradesmen, backed by the government of a country within a hairsbreadth of bankruptcy – a government rotten with corruption and place-seeking.'

'Oh, come now, Billy!' protested the Secretary uncomfortably. 'At least it's loyal—'

'To succeed in their invasion of this island,' Pitt continued unheeding, 'the French need only to gain control of the Channel for twenty-four hours. That control a victorious Dutch fleet can give them. And ship for ship the Dutch vessels are newer, better found, better manned, than our worn-out hulks. The odds are heavy against us.'

'Hold there, sir!' Dundas, who was Treasurer of the Navy as well as Secretary of State for War, arrested the refilling of his friend's glass to make forcible protest. 'At worst it's evens. D'ye forget St. Vincent, only eight months ago?'

With a touch of condescension Pitt abandoned his oration to reply. 'No. I forget nothing. Lord St. Vincent has my respect, but in that battle he commanded our finest ships and our finest men. He was opposed to Spaniards. However they may rate their ships, the Spaniards, like the French, will ever be second-rate powers at sea.'

'Jervis beat the Dons, all the same,' Dundas persisted.

'Four Spanish Ships of the line taken,' the Prime Minister said bleakly. 'The rest, back in Cadiz harbour, making ready for further battles. The Dutch, Hal, are far more dangerous. And they are at sea – which must mean that the French are ready, waiting only for the signal to invade, the message from their precious Batavian Republic that our North Sea Fleet has been made incapable of defending our shores.'

'Ye know well my agents have sent no word—'

'Your spies have failed us before. If the Dutch are out of the Texel there can be but one reason for it.'

Pitt dismissed the matter with a wave of his hand and took a gulp of port. He stood up a trifle unsteadily, his left hand planted flat on the table and his right outstretched for the over-dramatic gestures that so amused the Opposition wits. His voice rose again in bitter declamation.

'Our past sins indeed rise against us in the hour of danger, sins of omission and commission. The Dutch are at sea! We oppose to them the scrapings of our prisons, the children of our neglect, with an old man – undistinguished, almost unknown – to lead them into battle! That it should have come to this, my friends – that England should have come to this!' He swayed perilously and recovered himself. 'I have tried to show the way of salvation. I have tried to set the example – God knows I have tried. And I have failed. England alone remains to save Europe. And now – and now—'

His voice slowed and faded. A tear trickled down his haggard cheek. The thin hand gave a final helpless gesture and he sat down with a thump that all but overbalanced his chair. Dundas got up and came round the table, carrying the bottle. Billy was sometimes inclined to be gloomy until he'd passed the sixth glass.

'Na, na, man, haud your havering,' he said in his broadest Scots. 'They'll no' beat Adam Duncan, ye'll see.'

He splashed port into Pitt's glass.

'*Sapientia vino obumbratur,*' mumbled the Prime Minister thickly; but he drank deep.

Half-an-hour later a belated labourer, trudging past the Wimbledon villa through the windy darkness, heard a thin discordant singing and glanced up at the red curtain of the window. Two unmusical voices were giving a mawkish rendering of *Britons Strike Home*. The labourer passed on with a grin and a shake of his head; it was not the first time he had heard Mr. Pitt and his bottle-crony in song. To any English mind it was a comfort to know that the rulers of England had their human vices.

It was long after midnight when Manson, Mr. Pitt's stolid factotum, was wakened from a doze by the loud ringing of the bell in the parlour. Mounting the stairs and entering discreetly, he was surprised to find a reversal of the usual order of things; it was Mr. Dundas who snored in a heap under the table, while his master sat slumped in his chair gazing at vacancy. The fire had gone out. The guttering candles showed the Prime Minister's face deathly pale. Pitt, without altering his fixed stare, made a slight gesture towards the stertorous heap. Manson took expert hold under the Secretary's armpits and dragged him away to his bed, unaware that the closing of the parlour door had extinguished the fainting candles.

In the darkness Pitt sat on, and the darkness had pictures for him. He saw the great ships locked in battle, the flame and the smoke, the grey surge of the shallow waters where De Winter's vessels could manoeuvre safely while the English ships with their deeper draught must ground, and lie helpless, and strike or be pounded to splinters. He spoke at last, in an unsteady whisper that seemed to end a train of gloomy thoughts.

'And an old man to lead them into battle. God help them. God help Engand.'

Outside the house the wind roared among the dying leaves.

# ONE

## 1

The man stood by the rail of the flagship's stern gallery, looking into the night that hid the receding English coast. He stood erect, his big hands grasping the carved oak of the rail; a giant of a man, nearly six-and-a-half feet tall and broad in proportion. Standing upright required the bending and flexing of his right knee, for His Majesty's ship *Venerable* was laid on the larboard tack to beat against the gusty wind that blew from a little east of north-east, and heeled as she lifted on the short North Sea waves. There was wind enough to set them showing their white teeth, those waves, as they fled away astern into the blackness on either hand – a foul wind, indeed, for a fast passage to the Texel but far better than light airs or no wind at all. A few minutes ago the double clangs of the ship's bell, muted unevenly by the gusts, had come to his ears from the poop overhead: eight bells of the first watch. In thirty-six hours, perhaps twenty-four if the wind backed, he might be bearing down on De Winter's fleet. And then, thought Adam Duncan, then would come the test.

Those first few minutes of the morning, on October 10th in the year 1797, made Duncan feel that he was indeed an old man. The recurrent fever he had contracted at Havana thirty-five years ago had made a brief reappearance while *Venerable* was refitting at Yarmouth, and it could have been this that lowered his usually equable spirits; or the hour and the darkness might be weighing upon him. For his big, somewhat heavy face wore a frown as he stared out above the spreading grey-white wake that flowed from the flagship's stern thirty feet below him. Sixty-six. He had exceeded a man's expectation of life some years ago. Such burdens as his shoulders had been required to bear had been, by God's mercy, singularly light. Adam Duncan was accustomed to remember God's mercy when he looked back on his past life; a lifelong Presbyterian, he inclined to a Calvinistic view of predestination, and – particularly of late – saw himself as a vessel steered by a surer hand than his own. Now his course was set for the climacteric test of his whole life. And though Providence had already decided whether or not he should find De Winter's ships, he could not rid himself of the conviction that the result of any engagement depended, under Providence, upon himself.

It was late indeed to burden him with so vast a responsibility – too late, they would say if he failed to support it. That such a failure would break him, end his naval career, meant nothing; his career was already at an end, with retirement and one of Mr. Pitt's inexhaustible Irish Peerages looming ahead, probably before Christmas. He had told them more than once that he considered it his duty to remain in the Service as long as the war should continue, but he knew well enough that they had made their decision: he was too old.

He shook his massive head like a dog pestered by flies. The movement sent his thick white hair across his eyes and he dashed it aside with a rare gesture of impatience; it had never been his way to allow the opinions of others to influence his course once it was plain before him, nor had he ever sought a favour from those who could have advanced him in the Navy. The course before him now was very clear, if he could only hold it to the end – to find and engage the Dutch fleet, to destroy it utterly. Whether they had sailed to occupy the Channel Islands as one British agent had reported, or to seal off the Channel while the French invasion army crossed, made no difference; if they succeeded in either it would mean that England lay at the mercy of the invader. The fate of his country, the fate of Europe, hung upon the result of the sea battle that must now be fought, and the result of the battle depended upon him, Adam Duncan, Admiral of the Blue. And, of course, on God's will. He raised his eyes to the clouded night sky, beyond which he conceived his God to dwell, and prayed briefly but fervently that he might be found a worthy instrument of victory.

There was no vain inflation of self-importance in thus seeing himself as the man on whom all depended. The chance of victory hung not only on his skill and seamanship in command, but also on the loyalty with which his ships and his men followed him. Invisible in the darkness, ten ships of the line were beating eastward in company with *Venerable*, with upwards of five thousand men in them, men who had very recently learned the power of their numbers. At Spithead, at the Nore, crews had mutinied and taken over their ships, had proposed to blockade the Port of London, had fired on ships that sought to obey Admiralty orders. That was little more than four months ago, and it was obvious that seamen who disliked their commander or their objective would remember how easily they could abandon both. Even now there was doubt in Duncan's mind as to whether the five ships he had left refitting at Portsmouth and the Nore would join him or refuse to sail. He was aware, though the thought was repugnant to him, that the regard in which some thousands of seamen held their Admiral was a major factor in determining the outcome of the coming battle; that Europe's fate hinged, whether he liked it or not, on the character and actions of one man – himself.

'By'r leave, sir.'

The Admiral turned sharply, jerked from his reflections by the high Scots voice with its rolled R's. The gaunt figure of Menzies, his steward, stood at his elbow.

'Starb'd watch is on deck ten minutes syne, sir,' said Menzies severely. 'It's past midnight.'

'Very good,' snapped Duncan; and then, softening his deep voice, 'Thank you, Menzies. You can turn in. I'll see myself to bed.'

'Aye aye, sir,' grunted Menzies in a resigned tone.

He went in through the stern gallery door, and Duncan returned with a sigh to his contemplation of the ship's wake. Even Menzies had begun to treat him like a dotard, he realized. Was he indeed an old man? His strength was as great as ever it was, his sight and hearing excellent. He cocked his ear to the familiar multitudinous noises of the sea and the ship – the hiss and roar of waves, the creaking of the great rudder in its pintles beneath his feet, the thousand voices of block and rigging and straining canvas. He loved them now, even after the months of surfeit on the Texel blockade, as he had loved them when they were a heart-stirring novelty to a tall young midshipman from Dundee, fifty – no, fifty-one years ago. The sea road had opened ahead of him before then, though. He remembered a brilliant day in June 1744, with Spithead all a-sparkle and Anson's ship, sole survivor of the squadron which had set out to circumnavigate the world, coming slowly in under topsails. Thirteen years old he had been, on a visit to London with his father the Provost of Dundee, when they had taken coach to Portsmouth for that occasion. Half-a-million pounds in Spanish treasure; that was Anson's prize, so they said. A half smile deepened the lines on the Admiral's weather-beaten face as he recalled the boy's excitement, his instant ambition to emulate Anson and hunt down the Spanish treasure-ships. Little treasure his fifty-one years in the Navy had brought him, fifteen of them ashore on half-pay! But he had garnered other treasure, of diverse kinds; knowledge of himself and of men; knowledge of man's brutality and the sea's impersonal cruelty, with their balancing riches of fortitude and wild beauty; knowledge of duty well done. Perhaps the last had been the most fully satisfying. He had never thirsted for 'glory', as many of his fellow sea-officers had done; to Adam Duncan glory had seemed another name for self-aggrandisment. Instead, it had been his especial pride to do rather more than might be expected of him – and to keep such doings to himself.

He leaned on the rail, deliberately invoking a flood of memories to drown his nagging apprehensions of the future. The chill October wind, caught inward by the back-draught of the flagship's passage, plucked at his white locks and numbed his ears and fingers with its touch, but he scarcely felt it. He was a boy again, making his first cruise in the sloop *Tryal*, northabout from Inverness to search the Western Isles for Charles Edward and the broken remnants of the '45. In Robert Haldane, captain of the *Tryal* and his cousin, young Adam had found a hero to worship – and a first disillusion. Captain Haldane had taken his midshipman relative with him when he was given the frigate *Shoreham* at the end of that year and ordered on an independent cruise off the French coast. Sixteen years old, and his first chase and capture – a brig out of Brest, outgunned and easy prey; that had been a disappointing business, he remembered. Seven weeks later had come the affair at Belleisle with a French privateer. He thought of it now as his initiation into manhood, and even the date of the action – February 24th, 1748 – was clear in his mind.

Far away in Wimbledon Mr. Pitt was tormenting himself with pictures conjured on to the screen of darkness. Admiral Duncan, too, made pictures in the dark; but his were brighter, for he saw them with the eyes of youth. A steel-grey sea, *Shoreham's* bowsprit thrusting and lifting through the spray-showers, a long thin sword of winter sunshine touching to dazzling white the canvas of the flying vessel three miles ahead of the frigate....

## II

'We're closing her fast, Bonney,' shouted Captain Haldane over his shoulder; he snapped his telescope shut and leaped down to the deck from the weather-shrouds where he had been clinging precariously.

Bonney, his stocky sailing-master, shook a grizzled head. 'Not fast enough, sir, I fear.' He squinted at the scrawlings on the traverse-board. ' 'Cording to my reckoning, Quiberon's a bare three leagues on the larboard bow – due east.'

The young captain's swarthy face creased in a scowl. It was his foible to be annoyed when his enthusiasms were damped, no matter how reasonably. Still frowning, he peered impatiently up at the taut curve of the spanker straining at its tackle above the quarterdeck. The frigate was carrying every stitch of canvas she could wear; courses, topsails, and topgallants on main and foremasts, her huge jib bellying from the jibboom high over the bows, mizzen topsail spreading overhead beyond the spanker's tilted yard. The wind, a fresh sou'westerly, was a little abaft the beam – her best point of sailing. There was not another half-knot to be got out of her.

'Main braces!' he yelled suddenly. 'Haul away! – Well! I said "Well," damn you!'

The half-dozen seamen, clad in a motley assortment of jackets and tarpaulins, made fast the sheet. Taking in six inches of mainsheet would make little or no difference to the ship's speed, but it relieved Haldane's annoyance and made him feel superior to his sailing-master. He turned to Bonney with a grin that showed very white teeth.

'We'll engage her yet, if she's running for Quiberon Bay,' he said cheerfully. 'What's her force, d'ye think?'

'Much the same as ours, sir,' Bonney answered, rubbing the grey bristle on his chin. 'These Bay privateers carry twenty guns – more, sometimes.'

Haldane glanced for'ard along the deck, where the twelve-pounders on their wooden carriages nuzzled the closed gunports, ten on each broadside. Roach, his First Lieutenant, was prowling along the slanting deck, craning his long neck over each gun in turn; Roach was always fussing anxiously over his guns.

'She'll outnumber us man for man, though,' pursued the master. 'You'll never find a Brittany privateer that isn't crammed as full as she'll hold. Three hundred at least, I'd say.'

The frigate, already leaning far over to larboard, lurched slightly and recovered with a brief rattle of blocks. Haldane swung on his heel to shout at the seaman gripping the spokes of the big wheel.

'Confound you – steer small, or I'll have you flogged!' The quartermaster ducked his head guiltily under the captain's glare. Haldane resumed his conversation with Bonney.

'Odds of two to one against us – but in our favour when t'others are Frenchmen. God send us a chance of boarding her!' He turned to the other occupant of the quarterdeck, the midshipman of the watch. 'That'll be your chance, Mr. Duncan. I believe you've never wielded a cutlass?'

'No, sir,' said the midshipman stolidly.

He made a somewhat odd contrast with his captain, being several inches taller (though, at sixteen years old, he was seven years younger than Haldane) with a round rosy face and an almost statuesque poise. Compared with his senior officer, his dress was a model of perfection – waistcoat and white breeches spotless, blue cutaway coat creaseless over his wide shoulders, a small cocked hat perched neatly on hair well powdered and tied in a queue with black ribbon; Haldane's breeches were streaked with tar from the rigging and the tarpaulin jacket that hid his gold-braided coat was carelessly buttoned and flapped in the wind. Judging by manner and expression alone, an observer might have taken the captain for the younger of the two, for Robert Haldane's perpetual restlessness, the hint of swagger in his movements and gestures, and the liveliness of his hot brown eyes, were more suggestive of immaturity than his young cousin's impassive grey stare and rather ponderous actions. His lithe figure, too, looked boyish beside Adam Duncan's obvious brawn and muscle.

'I doubt a two-handed sword would suit you better,'

Haldane said with a grin. 'Sailing-master, can we find one for Mr.—'

'De-e-eck, there!'

The faint seagull-screech from the foremast-head interrupted him.

'Deck, there! Land in sight!'

Bonney nodded and grunted resignedly. Captain Haldane swung himself down the ladder to the maindeck without touching its five steps with his boots, and ran for'ard until he stood beneath the main course.

'Whereaway?' he roared through his cupped hands.

'Fine on the stabb'd bow, sir.' A short pause; then – 'An' more land, sir, – or it's mebbe a cloud – to labb'd. On the bow, sir.'

The captain swore and turned on his heel. 'Mr. Duncan!'

The midshipman came down from the quarterdeck in less spectacular fashion than his commanding officer. 'Sir!'

'The fellow up there can't tell cloud from *terra firma.* Take my glass. Get aloft – fore t'gallant masthead – and see which it is. Take a good look at the chase while you're there.'

'Aye aye, sir.'

'And look sharp!' Haldane yelled after him as he went for'ard at a slow trot. 'Never mind splitting your breeches!'

Adam Duncan maintained his steady lope, aware that his enormous stride took him the better part of a fathom at every step – as fast as most men could run. The groups of seamen standing ready at the tackles were grinning at the captain's remark about his breeches, but he did not mind. With his boundless admiration of his cousin, whom he considered the *beau idéal* of a dashing sea-officer, he was content to be the occasional butt of his jokes. He pulled himself on to the weather rail beside the foremast shrouds and began to climb them. The topfore platform loomed above his head with the futtock-shrouds stretching down and inward from it. Either Morris or Gaunt, his fellow midshipmen, would have climbed upward up the futtock-shrouds, back downwards above the deck below, to gain the foretop; Duncan's characteristic dislike of 'showing-off' made him drag himself up through the lubber's hole close to the mast. The stiff curve of the fore topgallant sail was like the inside of an enormous white globe on his right hand as he climbed steadily up to the masthead. Benskin, the lookout, was sitting astride the yardarm a dozen feet out from the crosstrees, one naked foot resting on the bellying canvas. He pointed to leeward and yelled something that was inaudible, whipped away by the roar of the wind. Duncan nodded at him, settled himself with his legs over the yard and one arm hooked round the topgallant mast, and pulled out the telescope from the tail pocket of his coat.

Directly beneath him, a hundred and fifty feet below, was the white-flecked sea sliding away astern. From up here the deck looked surprisingly narrow, the hull far too slender to support this thin tower of spars and their straining canvas. And whereas it had seemed, on the quarterdeck, that *Shoreham* was maintaining her heel to larboard evenly, it now appeared that the foremast was swaying, circling widely, perennially jerking as if it were trying to catapult him off one side or the other. Seven months at sea with his full share of mastheading had accustomed the boy to all this. He clamped the telescope to his eye and tried to steady it on the dancing horizon.

Being a boy, he looked first for the enemy, catching the white sails at last in a series of jerky glimpses. She was much nearer, two miles at most; a big vessel for a Biscay privateer, rigged like a frigate. He could make out a white streak along her side and see the black dots of gunports in it, but it was impossible to count them. He swung the telescope a little to the right. Yes, that was land sure enough, a headland or an island, low-lying, grey-green on the steel-grey sea. And to the left of the chase land again, more distant; bringing the glass farther to the left he could discern the darker line still running right round to northward a fraction above the horizon. Undoubtedly that was the French mainland – enemy territory. Adam Duncan knew little about the French, except that they were enemies, whose ships the navy must capture or sink whenever it got the chance. He was dimly aware that King Louis had taken the wrong side in the matter of something called 'the Austrian Succession' which had started a war six or seven years ago, while he was still at school in Dundee; but causes loomed very distantly beside nearer and clearer things like his ship and his captain and his duty as a naval officer. On the score of geography, however, Adam was better informed – the geography of seacoasts and islands. Mr. Bonney held daily classes in navigation and pilotage for the three midshipmen, on deck in fair weather and below in foul, and these – a dreary return to the schoolroom for Gaunt and Morris – were meat and drink to the boy from Dundee.

'Pointe de Conguel distant about eight miles, larboard bow,' he muttered as he stowed the glass in his tail pocket again. 'Belleisle fine on the starboard bow, less than five miles.'

He nodded to Benskin, swung effortlessly round on to the topmast shrouds, and clambered smoothly down to the deck. Captain Haldane, waiting impatiently on the quarter-deck, received his report with a scowl.

'Closing in to Belleisle, is he?' he growled. 'Why the devil doesn't the damned Frog run for Quiberon Bay?'

Midshipman Duncan, unwisely, supplied the obvious answer. 'We're overhauling him sir, and he won't give us the chance of coming in cannon-shot. Le Palais – that's on the nor'-east coast of Belleisle, sir – is a fortified port. Not a doubt but he's making for there, and once he's under the guns of the forts—'

'God help the navy when midshipmen take to strategy!' snapped Haldane irritably. 'Well, Mr. Bonney?'

'I'd say Mr. Duncan's right, sir. The privateer's out of Quiberon, surely, but there's a bare chance we'd catch him before he won to shelter. It'll be Le Palais he's headed for, right enough.'

The captain swore luridly (it was the one trait his young cousin found unheroic in him) and took a few jerky steps away and back again.

'What d'ye know of this place Le Palais?' he barked at the master.

Bonney massaged his bristly chin. 'I was there in the old *Swiftsure*, ten – nay, eleven – years ago. Good anchorage. Cliffs above the town, both sides, and big stone forts on 'em. Eighteen-pounders they had then. Some fellow name of Fouquet made it a rare strong place last century and it's been kept—'

'Eighteen-pounders, eh?' Haldane frowned.

'One salvo could sink us, sir. You could say she's safe already. Shall I – um – go about, sir?'

'Go about! God damme, Mr. Bonney, d'ye think I'll give up? Sail her as she goes, or I'll know the reason why.'

'Aye aye, sir,' said Bonney expressionlessly.

The frigate threshed on through the Biscay waves, while the February afternoon darkened fast towards evening. The south-wester held steady, the triangle of white canvas ahead grew larger as twilight crept across the clouded sky. By four bells of the first dogwatch, when Midshipman Gaunt relieved Midshipman Duncan on the quarterdeck, the coast of Belleisle was abeam, barely two miles away to starboard, and the French privateer was less than half that distance ahead; but in the rapidly fading light the enemy's sails and the wind-whipped sea and the low green pastures above the island's shore were only diverse shades of a grey monochrome.

Duncan wolfed a supper of biscuit and salt pork, washed down with a leathern mugful of small beer, in the tiny gun-room. As he gulped the last of the beer the boatswain's pipes shrilled. The piercing call was followed by the queer muffled roar of a hundred pairs of bare feet hurrying on deck, and by the time the midshipman emerged from the after hatchway H.M.S. *Shoreham* was trembling to the running-out of her twenty guns. Captain Haldane, it appeared, still nourished hope of an action. Duncan's own action station was for'ard in charge of the four bow guns. Roach's harsh tenor voice was reporting 'All guns loaded and run out' as he reached it, and the gun crews were staring ahead at their quarry. He did the same.

The Frenchman, so close that even in the twilight he could make out the changing set of her sails, was bearing up to round a dark headland that was the spur of higher ground behind the coast to starboard. A flash, startlingly bright, came from her deck and was followed shortly by a dull report.

'Defyin' us, like,' observed the gunlayer of Number One gun beside him.

Duncan said nothing, but he knew the gun had been fired to alert the batteries of Le Palais. Now the privateer, close-hauled, was sliding out of sight beyond the headland. *Shoreham* swept on, with less heel now that she was in the lee of Belleisle, in the wake of her quarry. The headland glided past, a black snout with white teeth. A long dimly-seen bay opened ahead, and suddenly, quite close on the right, a chain of twinkling lights at the sea's edge. There was a brief red flame, and then another, from the darkness above the chain of lights. Adam Duncan heard the crescendo scream of the eighteen-pounder balls passing overhead and was horribly afraid; but he restrained himself from ducking. The heavy double boom of the guns sounded as he discerned the privateer speeding into sanctuary.

Again two guns fired from the forts of Le Palais – the flashes farther to the left this time – and then another double flash where the first had been. Four eighteen-pounders. A grey column of water rose like a ghost from the sea not twenty fathoms from where he stood gripping the rail. Aft on the quarterdeck he could hear voices; one was Mr. Bonney's, seemingly raised in urgent protest. Adam gulped in excitement, wondering whether his dashing cousin was going to hold on after his prey, to take *Shoreham* in under the fire of the batteries. It would be tremendous, heroic, in the manner of the Berserkers. He felt that queer madness, the hot desire to follow his hero to death, for a moment only before his real self took charge and told him that the thing would be a useless and criminal folly.

'Hands to the braces!' That was Bonney's deep voice. 'Slack away – well! Make fast!'

The frigate was turning, but not towards the enemy. With the wind over her starboard quarter she drew to the eastward out of the bay, and none too soon. Two flashes in quick succession, from dead astern now, were followed by the vengeful screaming of the shot. There was a rending crash and the spanker hung flapping wildly from its shattered yard. Twice after that the eighteen-pounders fired, but with no more damage to *Shoreham*; the wind, strengthening once she was out of the lee of Belleisle, took her rapidly beyond their range.

Ten minutes later, with the lights of Le Palais invisible on the long black coast to larboard, she had worn and was heading back north-westerly through the dusk. The guns were secured, a working-party aft was unreeving the big sail from its broken yard. Captain Haldane came for'ard to where the gun crews stood awaiting dismissal.

'Very well, my lads,' he said coolly; though Midshipman Duncan could hear the pent anger in his voice. 'We run away to fight another day. For, by God, I'll have that Frenchman yet – take him, burn him, or scuttle him. Boatswain, pipe down.'

## III

Midshipman Adam Duncan sat in the sternsheets of the cutter with his big hand on the tiller and his eyes straining into the darkness ahead. It was four in the morning of the day following *Shoreham's* chase of the privateer. A thin rain blew down out of the night, and a short and lumpy sea was sending frequent showers of salt water over the starboard gunwale. Like the twelve seamen who pulled at the muffled oars, Midshipman Duncan was soaked to the skin; and – unlike them, since he had no physical work to do – he was very cold.

An hour ago the boats had pulled away from the frigate, leaving her anchored in nine fathoms close in to the Belle-isle coast four miles west of the headland, near Le Palais. So far as could be seen in the overcast night, this part of the coast was uninhabited; Captain Haldane was completely confident that no alarm would be given and that the cutting-out operation he planned would take the French at Le Palais completely by surprise. *Shoreham*'s work being expected to include much boarding and taking of prizes, she carried two boats in addition to her longboat, and all three were being used in this venture. Haldane himself was in charge of the longboat – the midshipman could just see her, a dark nucleus on the dark water ahead – and Duncan, senior of the three midshipmen by service though not by age, had the cutter. The third boat, a small pulling-boat which Haldane was accustomed to call his gig, was third in the line, astern of the cutter, with Mr. Owen the second lieutenant at the tiller. Owen and his four seamen had the task of cutting the privateer's mooring-ropes as soon as she had been boarded; this, and his own orders to board with the cutter's crew on the Frenchman's larboard side, was all that Midshipman Duncan knew of the cutting-out plan. As the boats bucketed through the rain and darkness towards the invisible headland that could not be far ahead now, he was fighting against the doubts of that simple plan which persisted in assailing him.

That a British frigate captain, baulked of his prey in chase, would attempt to cut her out under cover of darkness was to be expected by anyone who knew the ways of

His Britannic Majesty's Navy. Would not these Frenchmen know those ways? Adam Duncan tried to put himself in the place of a Frenchman on Belleisle; the privateer captain, or the commandant of the garrison. Even if he didn't anticipate a night raid from the English warship he would certainly take precautions against the possibility. He would double the lookouts on the forts, have the eighteen-pounders loaded and the gunners at hand; there would be an anchor watch on board the privateer, boarding-nettings rigged out from her sides, a guard boat pulling round her through the hours of darkness. Captain Haldane counted on a surprise. 'They'll have seen that lucky shot of theirs bring down the spanker – they won't expect us back after that,' he had said. It was, of course, just possible that he was right. And though the rain squalls and the choppy sea might make it awkward to come alongide the privateer, the offshore wind was as fair as it could be for taking her out from the Le Palais anchorage. Haldane was determined to make a prize of her; there had been no more mention of burning or scuttling. Adam admired his cousin-hero for that determination. All the same—

The almost invisible longboat ahead was altering course to larboard. As the midshipman eased the tiller over he saw the loom of the headland in the obscurity, close on the starboard bow. Too close. Even through the rain-filled darkness he could make out the moving line of white at the base of the cliffs. But the gusty wind was their friend here, pushing the boats clear of rock and shoal while they wallowed round the point. Adam turned to look astern, shuddering involuntarily as his drenched clothing dragged clammily on his flesh. He could see nothing of Mr. Owen's boat, which must be tricky to handle in these steep, lopping-over waves; but the important thing was that the longboat and the cutter should not lose touch with each other, so Mr. Owen would have to take his chance.

'Ten good ones, Lowry,' he said in a prematurely deep voice to the man who was pulling stroke on the larboard side.

That brought the cutter to within twenty fathoms' distance of the longboat's stern and made it easier for him to follow the captain's lead. The boats rocked and heaved through the joggle of conflicting currents off the tip of the headland for ten minutes and then the loom of the cliffs to starboard faded and they were breasting the steadier waves of the bay. There was no sign at all of the coast, unless you counted the rain-laden gusts which told of the wind funnelling down glens or clefts in the low hills behind Le Palais. Adam eased the tiller to larboard. Haldane was heading in towards the anchorage. Peer as he might, he could see nothing ahead except the squat shape of the longboat. He moved his foot below the stern thwart to assure himself that his cutlass was where he had stowed it; the pistol stuck in his belt, it could safely be assumed, would misfire when he pulled the trigger.

There was a definite lessening of the waves' violence now. They must be well into the anchorage – and there, at last, was a dim blur of yellow light, soon distinguishable as two separate lights, brightening and seeming to rise higher in the darkness as the boats approached: a vessel at moorings.

The lights had drawn Midshipman Duncan's attention from his leader, and he had barely time to mutter 'Hold water!' and starboard his helm before the cutter drew alongside the suddenly-halted longboat. The captain, he saw, was standing motionless in the sternsheets with his hand raised in an urgent gesture for silence. Through the slap of the waves and the hiss and patter of the rain came the sound of oars in rowlocks, fast growing louder. Right ahead, halfway between the boats and the double blur of light, a black shape moved across from left to right and disappeared. The lit ship was the privateer, sure enough; and they had a guard boat pulling round her.

Duncan released his pent breath and felt his heart thumping like the hoofbeats of a carthorse. It seemed incredible that the frigate's boats had not been seen – until he perceived that the guard boat had been visible to them only by the fortunate chance of its passing between them and the ship's lights. A fortunate chance? Or a 'sign' that this adventure was predestined, ordained to succeed – in spite of Robert Haldane – by Providence? Young Adam's inclination was towards the second theory.

Haldane spoke while the creak of oars could still be heard, in a low voice audible to every man.

'Straight in and board. No cheering, no firearms. Cold steel.' He turned his head. 'Mr. Duncan!'

'Sir?'

'Where's Mr. Owen's boat?'

'Well astern, sir. We lost touch west of the headland.'

'No matter,' Haldane muttered after a pause. 'Lead on – we'll give you ten seconds start.'

'Aye aye, sir. Cutter's crew, give way together.'

The fact that the privateer would be riding head to wind meant that her larboard side was the further side and the cutter had farther to go. Adam steered to pass wide of the left-hand light, which must be the poop lantern, and then swung the boat in a sharp turn to starboard.

'Now! Pull for your lives!'

He couldn't prevent his voice from shaking. If there was a guard boat there were sure to be nettings rigged. They'd dodged the one by luck but there'd be no dodging the nettings. The cutter was leaping through the water. Any moment now. There was a screech and a bang while the yellow glow of the lantern was still a few fathoms away.

'Boat oars! – Bows! – Up with you, lads!'

The cutter sheered alongside with a thump and a shuddering rasp that nearly upset the midshipman as he groped for his cutlass. The bowman was trying desperately to hold her in while his shipmates leaped to the broad rubbing-strake and clutched for handhold. Duncan, exerting his long reach, grasped thin cordage overhead; the boarding netting. He slashed furiously with his cutlass, holding to the rim of a gun port with his left hand, and shifted his grasp to the severed ropes.

'Here, men! Follow!'

Bright flashes and deafening reports sounded overhead, and a pandemonium of shouting. The thrust of a boarding pike tore the cloth under his left armpit as he tumbled anyhow over the privateer's rail. He clamped it there with his arm and struck blindly with his cutlass-hilt at a dark figure in front of him. The figure vanished and another with outstretched arm took its place. An instant before the pistol exploded Duncan fell headlong, tripped up by the pike entangled in his coat. His shoulder crashed into the Frenchman's legs and the man fell on top of him. He heaved himself free and tore off his coat in time to fell his assailant with a sweeping blow as he staggered to his feet; and for the space of two breaths had time to look round him.

The yellow glow of the poop lantern, scarcely penetrating the rainy darkness, showed the deck a seething mass of dark figures whirling and striking and falling. Unmistakably British yells amid the uproar of shouts and screeches and pistol-shots told that the longboat's men had gained their footing on deck. (Could his cousin really have hoped to capture the ship in silence?) That there were so many men engaged in the mêlée must mean that the cutting-out party was hopelessly outnumbered. He had noted all this in one swift glance. Then he was heaved backwards by a blind rush of men jammed so close together that their blows at him were as ineffective as his at them. A knee thrust into someone's stomach – the man stank of garlic – freed him. He felt rather than saw British seamen at his side and together they thrust forward, striking and shouting until another rush forced them aft towards the poop, stumbling over dead or wounded men as they went. A knife sliced into Duncan's forearm; he cut savagely downward with his weapon and felt the blade jar on bone. Mad with excitement and the pain of his wound, he struck and thrust and struck again, the cutlass whipping like a malacca cane, until they gave back before him and the red mist cleared from before his eyes. There were men hurrying out of the midships hatchway. From his greater height he could see them over the swaying heads of the crowd, buttons and muskets glinting in the faint lantern-light. Soldiers from the garrison! This was the end, then. Their lucky evasion of the guard boat had merely let them into the trap they should have expected.

Another noisy rush. A swordstroke whistled past his ear. In dealing it his assailant had stumbled, and the blade crashed down on some wooden structure beside him – the coaming of the after hatch.

'*Shorehams!*' yelled Robert Haldane's voice, close to him. 'To me! Come on, and clear this—'

The yell ended in a groan. As half-a-dozen of the frigate's men hurled themselves forward, cheering hoarsely, the captain slumped against a seaman behind him. Now a shrill French voice rose above the tumult imploring the defenders to stand clear so that the soldiers could use their muskets; but for a moment its only effect was to confuse the French and weaken their pressure. In the moment's respite Midshipman Duncan thought fast, if confusedly.

Failure, utter and complete. Death or a French prison for all of them. The frigate, likely enough, would be surprised and taken – there'd be a Court Martial and disgrace for Robert Haldane, if he was still alive. The 'sign' he had thought to discern had not been for Haldane's success, after all. Haldane was down, and (he realized it with a shock) he, Adam Duncan, was in command now. Across his mind flashed recollection of the swordstroke that had just missed him. It had revealed that he was standing beside the after hatch—

'Sir!' A seaman – it was Lowry – was clutching at his wounded arm. 'The cutter, sir – she's sunk. Frogs dropped a roundshot through 'er bottom.'

There was still the longboat. By sheer fury the *Shoreham's* men had driven the mass of Frenchmen backwards on to the line of soldiers, who were struggling with ramrods and powderhorns, but they were being forced slowly aft again. There was a last slim chance. Lowry, if shorter than himself, was broader and immensely strong.

'Get Captain Haldane into the longboat, Lowry,' he said rapidly. 'Pull clear as soon as the men are aboard. You, Taylor –' he addressed the man who was supporting the captain – 'come with me.' He raised his voice to its full pitch, a deafening bellow. '*Shoreham* men! 'Bandon ship! The longboat – starboard side!'

Then he turned and flung himself down the ladder of the after hatch, with Taylor at his heels.

In the alleyway at the foot of the ladder a horn lantern burned dimly, hanging on the bulkhead. Duncan saw the man skulking in the shadows beyond it and ducked aside as the pistol exploded. Two strides and he had the Frenchman by the scruff of the neck and the cutlass-blade against his throat. But when he looked back he saw Taylor's body crumpled on the deck below the swaying lantern, whose light showed the ragged black hole in the seaman's forehead.

Sorrow and vengeance were alike outside his present plan. The French he had acquired as a normal part of a gentleman's education had not included sea terms, but he could make his needs plain enough.

'*Au dessous!*' he growled threateningly at his prisoner.

Growl and cutlass were sufficient for the skulker. He pointed a shaking finger along the alleyway. The midshipman tore the lantern from its gimbals and forced the man forward at a trot with the cutlass-point; down a second ladder at the alleyway's end; past the cable-tier into the stinking darkness of the hold, where the Frenchman stopped with a flurry of gestures and feverish protest.

'*Au dessous!*' said his captor sternly. 'Sea-cock, man – where's the sea-cock? *Compris?*'

That the man understood was plain. His thin face showed horror, but he pointed, indicating a wooden handle in a round iron casting set low in the slanting planks which were the ship's side below the waterline. As Duncan bent over the handle the Frenchman hurled himself upon him, clawing and spitting like a cat, and was flung off to lie groaning six feet away. A steady pull, a quarter-turn – and the waters of the Bay of Biscay were spouting into the hold.

The volume and power of the thing he had released astonished the midshipman, so that he stood for a moment staring at the horizontal column of water emerging from the opened cock and jetting far across the dark hold to roar down on the timbers. The Frenchman had seized his chance and was away up the ladders to give the alarm. But no one was going to close this sea-cock. Duncan set down the lantern and braced himself with his legs straddling the jet of water so that he could exert his full strength in an outward pull. His great muscles swelled, cracked – and the handle snapped off at its junction with the ring of the cock.

The rising water was lapping the base of the lantern when he picked it up. He climbed fast up the ladder and ran along the alleyway. A burst of firing – pistols and muskets – came from the deck above and assured him that the longboat had won clear, or at least had a chance of doing so; and he wondered, for the first time, whether Robert Haldane was on board, whether Robert was dead or alive. His concern, now, was for a cousin; not for a worshipped hero, for that hero had revealed himself a rash unthinking fool.

A man came leaping down the ladder just as Duncan stepped over Taylor's body. He hurled the lantern at him and charged like a bull, taking him at the knees and sending him flying over his shoulder. The neighbourhood of the after hatchway was clear when he raised his head cautiously above the coaming. He could hear the alleyway skulker screeching his urgent news, but every man on deck was crowding against the starboard rail or on the poop and no one seemed to be taking any notice of him. They were firing after the departing longboat and yelling at the same time, after the manner of Frenchmen.

Midshipman Duncan loped unseen to the larboard rail, hauled himself on to it – painfully, because of his wounded arm – and plunged over the side. The Tay surges had made him a strong swimmer before he had reached his teens, but it was long before his shouts halted the longboat and he was exhausted when they hauled him aboard.

'Give – way there, men,' he panted as soon as he could speak; musket and pistol were still banging away on board the privateer.

'All right, sir – we're out o' range 'ere.' Seaman Lowry had shipped his oar and was binding a rag round Duncan's arm as he spoke. 'Thought you was lorst, sir.' He hesitated. 'The guard boat took Mr. Owen, sir – saw 'em do it as we went overside. An' there's eleven of us in the longboat, countin' two Frenchies as jumped in after us. Jones batted 'em over the 'ead an' they're stowed in the bows.'

'And the captain?'

'Cap'n 'Aldane's 'ere, sir, down in the sternsheets. Bullet across the side of 'is 'ead, an' not feelin' all that good.'

'Adam?' Haldane's voice was faint. 'Thank God you're safe—'

'Look at that!' exclaimed one of the oarsmen, interrupting his captain without ceremony. 'The privateer – she's took a list!'

Duncan noticed then that the firing had ceased entirely. He turned to gaze astern. The thin rain was still falling, but a pallor of dawn was spreading across the low clouds and darkness was lightening to charcoal grey. He could see the black shape of the privateer plainly. Her masts were tilted sharply over and she was very low in the water. A medley of shouts and screeches came to his ears. The confused activity on the surface near her suggested that she was being hastily abandoned.

'Mr. Duncan!' Haldane said feebly. 'Why are we not under way?'

'Aye aye, sir. Give way together, men.'

The longboat, gathering speed slowly, headed to round the dark headland beyond which *Shoreham* awaited them.

'A bad business,' Haldane was muttering as if to himself; the faint voice sounded bitter. 'I'll be broke for this. Everything went awry—'

'According to the plan, sir.' Duncan spoke loudly, drowning the captain's last word. 'You scuttled the privateer, as was proposed. Taylor was killed doing it – and brought off two prisoners.' He cleared his throat. 'A very successful operation, sir, if I may say so.'

# TWO

## I

A single deep clang sounded from high overhead on *Venerable*'s elaborately carved poop: one bell of the Middle Watch. Admiral Duncan, returning to the present with a start, realized that he was chilled to the bone. He was smiling to himself, all the same, as he went in through the door of the stern gallery. Midshipman Duncan had been inclined to think himself rather a fine fellow after that Belleisle business. He had told no one of his doings in the hold of the privateer, and Captain Haldane had been content to credit himself with scuttling a dangerous enemy ship in an enemy harbour and bringing off two prisoners; thus, curiously enough – for this had been the object of the boy's actions – toppling finally from the pedestal on which Adam Duncan had placed him. Nor had Cousin Robert profited by the lesson his young relative had read him. In that same year he had allowed *Shoreham* to run aground on the German Rock, in Plymouth Sound, and the Court of Inquiry that followed resulted in Captain Robert Haldane losing his command.

A ghostly figure that could have been Menzies hovering fussily in the alleyway vanished as the Admiral entered his sleeping cabin. The dim light of the oil-lamp gyrating slowly in its gimbals seemed brilliant compared with the darkness of the gallery and the cabin smelt warm, even stuffy. He sat down heavily on his cot (it had been specially constructed to take his immense length and weight) and began to take off stockings and breeches, grunting as he bent stiffly, adjusting his balance to the leisurely sway of the ship. Tomorrow night he would sleep fully dressed, if he slept at all. It crossed his mind, as he pulled over his head the warm flannelette nightgown Henrietta had made for him, that this might be his last night's sleep on earth. The thought did not greatly perturb him, except that it renewed his anxieties about the outcome of the battle with the Dutch.

He pulled the blankets round his ears with a sigh that

was half a groan of relief and lay still, with an occasional shiver, listening to the ship's thousand voices. It was far noisier here than on the deck of the stern gallery. The bulkheads and the deckhead above acted like sounding boards for the wind's thrumming in shrouds and rigging, and *Venerable* – an old ship – creaked in all her timbers with every lift and 'scend of the hull. But his years of service had accustomed him to sleeping through the uproar of the 'tween decks in a ship at sea. *Centurion* and *Torbay*, particularly the latter, had been hardly less noisy than *Venerable*. The old *Torbay* – he had loved that ship; but she had typified the ill fortune that had dogged his naval career. Climbing slowly, year by year, up the ladder of routine promotion, he had been transferred from *Torbay* just before she embarked on that glorious career under Sir Edward Hawke wherein every officer on board had earned distinction. He had been a Commander then, with his name ready to go forward for captain's rank after fourteen years in the Navy. But it had not been ill fortune that brought him, two years later, into *Valiant* as Commodore Keppel's Flag Captain.

The Admiral shifted uneasily and wriggled his toes. He was taking a long time to get warm tonight. It had been incautious to expose himself so long on the stern gallery without his boat-cloak when the fever was still lurking in his bones, feeble though that last attack had been. He remembered how he had shaken with cold when it had first struck him down, in the sweaty heat of midsummer 1762 on the north coast of Cuba; how the sneering face of Colonel Pawling had haunted his deliriums, and how he had feebly tried to exorcize it by conjuring up the vision of Keppel's serene, pale countenance. Strange, perhaps, that a thirty-year-old Flag Captain should still need a hero to worship; but Commodore the Honourable Augustus Keppel was a very different kind of hero from Captain Robert Haldane. Continuously racked by the pains of gout and rheumatism, smitten by the fever that was killing an average of two seamen a day on board *Valiant* and five times that number in the shore camp, the Commodore preserved his tranquil ordering of affairs without a sign of weakness. Only his Flag Captain could guess at the fortitude that held the tortured man so calm and competent while the siege of Havana dragged on into its fourth week and yellow fever slew three men for every one that was killed by a Spanish bullet. But for Keppel's example, reflected the Admiral as he lay on his swaying cot aboard his own flagship, the Flag Captain might never have got himself ashore that July morning at Havana; might never have performed the one action of his life that could be called bravado....

## II

'Captain, sir! Captain – *sir*!'

Captain Duncan heard the voice as from a great distance and strove to open his eyes, which were glued shut by their gummy exudations. The midshipman who had entered his cabin spoke again as he succeeded in getting his eyelids apart.

'Commodore's compliments, sir, and he'd be obleeged if you'd go to his cabin.'

'Very good,' muttered Duncan, sitting up on his cot.

He felt utterly weak; where his spine should have been there seemed to be no support, only an insupportable ache. He would have collapsed on his cot again if the midshipman had not been still in the cabin, staring at him with something like horror.

'Thank you, Mr. Wishart,' he made himself say gruffly, and the boy departed hurriedly.

Duncan swung his legs over the side of the cot, narrowly avoiding kicking over the bucket containing his vomit. It was nearly black, he noticed with disgust. The steward ought to have cleared that away – but with officers as well as men sickening daily of this horrible disease Merrick the surgeon had every non-fighting hand slaving for him all over the ship. There was a little water in a ewer on the sidetable. His wavering legs got him to it and he swilled his mouth out, not daring to drink lest it made him vomit again. The tiny mirror showed his face like a painted clown's, pallid and stained with great purple rings round each eye; no wonder Wishart had stared. He made a rapid toilet with his handkerchief dipped in water, swabbed the front of his shirt as best he could, forced trembling arms into the sleeves of his uniform coat and staggered out of the cabin.

The salute of the marine sentry outside his cabin door steadied him. He drew his big figure into its customary pose – erect to the chest, head and shoulders bowed to keep his head from striking the deckhead beams – and went aft along the alleyway. In his ears was the distant *boom . . . boom* of the siege guns pounding Fort Moro, and the nearer, fainter babel of human sound in the ship; men shrieking and jabbering in delirium, men groaning in the death throes. Twenty-three days and nights of those noises had accustomed Captain Duncan's ears to them; but this morning they seemed the accompaniment of some frightful hallucination. When he entered the great cabin and saw Keppel seated at the desk, the Commodore's slight form appeared to waver and duplicate itself and merge again in the most bewildering manner.

'Good morning, Captain.' Keppel's blanched face turned to him; the sunken eyes, grave and penetrating, half closed as he frowned. 'Sit down, Captain Duncan, if you please. Quickly.'

Duncan lurched forward, trying to control his wobbling knees, and managed to drop into the oaken chair opposite the desk without overturning it. Keppel eyed him for a long moment before he spoke.

'They have breached the north bastion at last, Captain.' His voice was low and even. 'A cutter from the flagship came alongside a few minutes ago with orders from the Admiral. Sir Robert wishes the *Valiant's* seamen to make the first assault. A senior officer from *Valiant* will be ashore to watch over the operation.' He hesitated briefly. 'You will go, if you please.'

'Aye aye, sir,' said Duncan; his voice seemed to belong to someone else.

The Commodore placed both hands on the desk and lifted himself with difficulty to his feet. The hands were ugly, every joint swollen and deformed with his disease. He limped to the stern window, which stood wide open on the vivid blue line of the Caribbean horizon; the sea lay dead calm, and the air entering the cabin did nothing to alleviate its oven-like heat.

'This must be considered an honour for *Valiant*, Captain,' said Keppel without turning from his contemplation of the distance. 'I shall be obliged if you will point that out to the men. My gig is waiting and will take you ashore. My compliments to Mr. Fisher and my wishes for a complete success.'

'Aye aye, sir.'

The haggard face was turned to him and Keppel's glance dwelt briefly on his Flag Captain's discoloured countenance.

'I have no need, Captain, to explain the situation,' he said expressionlessly. 'It will be as well if you do not delay.'

'Aye aye, sir,' said Duncan finally.

Apparently without his own volition, he was out on deck with the burning sun beating on his head. A mile away across the water to southward the low coastline of Cuba danced and shimmered, greenish brown dotted with the pale-brown marks which were the earthworks of the siege batteries. Puffs of smoke rose irregularly above the earthworks and were answered from the dark mass of Fort Moro on its pedestal of rock at the entrance of the lagoon. Opposite Moro, on the other side of the entrance, was the fortress called El Fuerte, and within the bottle-neck the Puntal batteries menaced any enemy vessel so incredibly lucky as to escape the guns of the forts; but Moro was the key to Havana, for once her commanding guns were in enemy hands and could be turned on her sister fortresses they must inevitably surrender. That would be the end of Havana, richest colonial possession of King Charles III of Spain – and a heavy blow to the confident Spaniards who had leagued themselves with France against Britain. To the left of the siege batteries a long bar of dingy white showed the encampment of the Army. It was a striking demonstration of sea power, that encampment. Within a few months of the declaration of war against Spain an army of 11,000 men had been transported half round the globe to attack the source of her enemy's wealth. Those who had planned the expedition had doubtless deemed it an overwhelming force; but they had underestimated the terrible power of Spain's ally, Yellow Jack.

Duncan turned from his brief contemplation of the scene, aware of someone fidgeting at his elbow.

'If you please, s-sir—' It was a nervous midshipman – 'Mr. Rennie bade me fetch you this, sir.'

He held out the captain's hat. Duncan took it from him with a mumbled word of thanks, rammed it on his head, and made himself walk firmly to the head of the gangway where the bosun's mate waited with the silver 'calls' at their lips to pipe him over the side. Only the realization that the gig's crew were watching him got him down the steps without stumbling and falling. He collapsed rather than sat down in the sternsheets, and the boat slid away from under *Valiant*'s towering wooden flank and headed for the shore.

The sun dazzled from right ahead on the shot-silk water and made him close his eyes; but he opened them again instantly, afraid of sinking into unconsciousness. He must prepare himself for taking charge, for making some sort of speech to the assault party, for polite meetings with the Army officers. He hoped he would not have to meet Pawling.

Keppel had said there was no need for him to explain the situation, and that was true enough as far as *Valiant* was concerned. The Flag Captain knew as well as his Commodore that he was the only officer who could go ashore on this mission; Barford the First Lieutenant was in command of the ship's shore detachment and would lead the assault on the breach, Rennie – the only other officer able to stand – had to remain on board as deck officer. But Keppel was not aware (for Duncan had not told him) of the troublesome friction with the Army which had begun on the very day of disembarkation. Duncan himself had been responsible for disembarking the troops, and the fact that Admiral Pocock had sent for him specially to commend his performance of the duty was proof enough that he had performed it well. Yet there had been caustic criticism from the Army in the person of the beach-head commander, Colonel Pawling. Pawling's antagonism towards the Navy and all its works appeared to be far stronger than his feeling against the Spanish foe. His collaboration with the naval captain in charge of the landing operation had consisted of a farrago of petty criticism and contemptuous comment, ending with certain remarks which a less equable sea officer might have taken as ground for a challenge and a duel. That the Navy was the senior service, and that Duncan was therefore the senior officer of the two although they were of equal rank in their respective services, had not helped matters; the Flag Captain had been forced to use that seniority twice in overruling suggestions of the Colonel's which did not fit in with his methodical arrangements, and Pawling had not concealed his fury. Pawling's weapon was sarcasm. Adam Duncan, who could not have been sarcastic if he had tried, was particularly vulnerable to it. In his present state he felt incapable of facing that barbed tongue again.

The ceaseless booming of the guns from fort and batteries was louder now. In the fifteen minutes it had taken the gig to reach the long slow rollers that bore her towards the beach Duncan had not consciously heard the sullen explosions; he had ceased to notice them now, as one ceases to hear the loud ticking of a clock. The gig plunged shoreward on the crests, the rows of tents on the beach well to the left of the nearest batteries appearing and disappearing ahead as she dipped and rose. Half a dozen bronzed seamen, stripped to the waist, ran into the surf to grasp her gunwales and run her up until she grounded. Tate, the Commodore's stalwart coxswain, got Duncan onto his shoulders and staggered with him through the hissing backwash to set him down dryshod, but the Captain's weight and awkward limpness confused the setting-down and he stumbled and fell with one knee in the wet sand. Tate helped him to his feet, apologetically.

A short rise of beach ended at the foot of a rank of low dunes that quivered bewilderingly in the heat. There were canvas awnings all along the base of the dunes, with hundreds of men – a few moving but most of them lying still – packed in the squares of blue shadow; the hospital tents beyond the dunes were full to overflowing. A track of boards had been laid up through a dip in the sandhills. At the top of it, within sight of the beach, stood a little group of officers in scarlet coats with one man a little in advance of the others. Undoubtedly that lean motionless figure with folded arms was Colonel Pawling. Duncan willed himself to move steadily up to him without swaying or stumbling, and succeeded.

'Good morning, sir,' Pawling said in the rasping drawl he affected, touching his hat at the precise instant when Duncan touched his. 'You are aware, I presume, that our – ' he gave a grating cough – 'that the guns have opened a breach.'

The hue of his fiery red face clashed unpleasantly with the colour of his uniform coat. He was tall and held himself erect, but his hot brown eyes were scarcely level with the Flag Captain's chin.

'Yes, sir,' said Duncan.

He was also aware that the guns constituted another annoyance for the Colonel; the battery manned by *Valliant*'s seamen had been able to fire three shots for every two fired by any Army battery.

'It is to be hoped, sir,' rasped Pawling, 'that the assault can now be made by your men.' He paused deliberately. 'We have been waiting this past hour to order the Cease Fire.'

'There shall be no further delay, sir. The assault party is in readiness?'

'I believe they consider themselves so, sir. Though I must inform you that your lieutenant—'

He checked himself. The Flag Captain's knees had given way beneath him as he strode resolutely forward, and he would have fallen on the hot sand but for the captain of Pawling's staff who caught his arm.

'You're unwell, sir?' The Colonel's tone was mock-solicitous. 'You'll find the climate here less comfortable than on board your ship. We, of course, are habituated to it. You can proceed?'

'It is nothing,' Duncan said shortly.

This wouldn't do. In his person he represented Keppel, the Admiral, the Navy. He thought he saw Pawling's aides grinning behind their hands. In his situation, he told himself, Keppel would have conquered his weakness and given these sweating redcoats no cause for amusement. He gathered himself together and went on with his long stride, half a pace ahead of the Colonel. The sand underfoot gave place to the bare and trampled earth of the camp, and the still air was at once heavy with an indescribable odour, the smells of latrines and stewed meat mingling with a predominant smell of sickness which spread from the massed tents and hutments two hundred yards away on the left. In front were some dozens of smaller tents, several with a redcoated sentry outside the doorway.

'I have had your lieutenant brought into one of these tents, sir,' Pawling said. 'The surgeon – I regret, but it has to be an Army surgeon who attends him—'

'What?' Duncan exclaimed, halting abruptly.

'I was about to inform you, sir. Mr. Barford was striken

with the fever this morning. He lies in the third tent of yonder row—'

'I must see him. Where is the naval detachment, Colonel?'

Pawling pointed to the right, where the level ground rose in a miniature of rock and earth above whose crest occasional filmy clouds of smoke rose and spread. The dull detonation of the cannonade came from the far side of the ridge, and down a broad track, littered with debris, came a thin trickle of men – hurrying messengers, limping wounded, stretcher-bearers.

'They are waiting behind the west battery, sir. They have been waiting the better part of an hour,' added the Colonel pointedly. 'I shall escort you—'

'I must see Mr. Barford first.'

'Confound it, sir! Are you not aware that this—'

But the Flag Captain was already striding towards the tents.

'I shall report this unnecessary delay, Captain Duncan!' Pawling snarled after him.

'Pray do so, Colonel,' said Duncan over his shoulder.

The sudden emergency seemed to have stiffened his joints. Barford out of it! That left Champerdown to lead the assault—

The little tent was stifling hot. A gaunt man in regimentals with his jacket unbuttoned was bending over a cot dabbing a wet cloth on the brow of the man who lay there.

'Mr. Barford!' Duncan said, stepping foward.

The army surgeon looked up. 'I doot he'll recognize ye,' he said dourly. 'At the secondary stage, as ye'll ken—'

'Captain!' said Lieutenant Barford faintly. 'The men – the assault – I can't—'

His voice died away. Duncan bent over him.

'Champerdown,' Barford whispered. 'Not fit. Never under fire. Scared—'

He struggled up on one elbow, retched violently, and vomited into the bowl the surgeon inserted neatly under his chin in the nick of time.

Duncan stood back. Champerdown was one of the junior lieutenants who had joined at Portsmouth. It had been made abundantly plain already that he was no leader of men.

The surgeon was laying Barford back on the cot. The

lieutenant's eyes were closed and though his stained lips writhed no sound came from them.

'Ye'll do more harm than guid here,' the surgeon said bluntly. 'The man's small chance enough withoot addeetional excitation.'

Duncan nodded. He spoke loudly.

'All will go well with the assault, Mr. Barford, never fear.'

As he turned to go dizziness seized him for a moment and he reeled, saving himself by a clutch at the fabric of the tent doorway. The surgeon scowled at him.

'Ye're in need of a doctor yoursel', man,' he said irritably. 'Sit ye doon – here's a wee stool—'

'I'm well enough.' Duncan steadied himself, holding to the shaking canvas. 'I have urgent duty.'

'Who will to Cupar, maun to Cupar,' said the surgeon, wagging his head; he groped beneath the cot and brought out a stout walking-cane. 'Ye'll find this useful, maybe.'

The Flag Captain hesitated. It might have been the familiar accent that decided him. With a muttered word of thanks he took the stick; and, bracing himself, walked out into the glare of sunlight.

## III

'Along the forward sap there, sir,' Colonel Pawling directed. 'That – ah – ditch, perhaps I should say, since the correct term may be unknown to you. Will you allow me to precede you?'

'Do so, sir, if you please.'

Pawling squeezed into a narrow trench running into the sandy soil of the rising ground facing them, and Duncan followed, leaning heavily on his stick. From above and in front came the ear-splitting bangs of Fort Moro's guns, mingled with the screech of the eighteen-pounder balls passing overhead and the lighter but more frequent explosions from the batteries.

The two officers, followed at a respectful distance by one of Pawling's aides, had come by the track over the ridge and past the emplacements where the sweating gunners laboured at their swabbing and loading and ramming – monotonous work but dangerous, for the shot from the fort was well directed. The iron balls thudded frequently into the earthworks or ploughed spurting furrows in the sandy turf behind them. Pawling stalked along in apparent oblivion of danger; his companion was concentrating all his powers on keeping pace with his guide and had no room in his mind for fear. Near *Valiant*'s battery (where the seamen gunners, stripped to the waist, raised an astonished cheer at sight of their captain) Pawling stopped to mount a step in an embrasure that gave a clear view of the objective. An army artilleryman lay hideously dead a few yards away, but the Colonel spared not a glance for the mangled body as he peremptorily beckoned the Flag Captain to stand beside him. Fort Moro loomed vast and squat on its low plinth of rock, tower and bastion jetting smoke and flame every few seconds. It was less than a quarter of a mile away from this viewpoint, and the line of chains and stakes and man-made clefts that ran across its rocky base could be clearly seen. At one point, however, these lower defences were destroyed, lost beneath an immense sloping mound of rubble that had fallen from above. There was a great gap in the wall, yawning wide where the cresting battlements had once been and narrowing down to a mere black fissure at the top of the mound of debris.

'The breach,' Pawling explained patronizingly. And, a minute or two later, 'We term this "dead ground" in the Army – I confess myself ignorant of the naval term.'

That was as the two, Pawling in the lead, passed quickly across a hillside ledge where no cannon-ball – except an unlikely dropping shot – could menace them. It had brought them to the narrow forward sap. Duncan, reeling doggedly along in the wake of the hurrying Colonel, calculated hazily that they must now be less than three hundred yards from the fort; the detonations of the guns shook the ground and set rivulets of earth pouring down the side of the trench. Men had died in the making of this forward sap. He observed with some disgust a detached human leg, which some jocular soldier had propped with rocks on the top of the lefthand parapet. Sweat was streaming off him and only the abnormal length of his stride enabled him to keep six feet behind the Colonel. The walking-stick given him by the surgeon was proving quite invaluable, for without it he would have fallen a dozen times – and perhaps been incapable of rising. But the purpose he had formed when he stood beside Barford's cot was like some powerful drug, giving him an inner strength that could force limbs that had no strength to do his will. The sense of action preordained was irresistibly upon him.

'Here, sir,' said Pawling with a scarcely-concealed sneer, 'is your assault party.'

The sap had curved round a massive limestone boulder and ejected them on a turfy shelf. A twelve-foot outcrop of rock ran along it on the south, hiding the fort overhead and sheltering from its fire the hundred and fifty seamen who sat or lounged all along the base of the outcrop. Lieutenant Champerdown, a gangling youth whose blue coat hung loosely from his shoulders, hastily called the men to attention and donned his hat before stepping forward to salute his captain. The saluting hand, Duncan noticed, was trembling. He ignored Champerdown's stammered report as he looked the double rank of seamen over. The Colonel's sneer could perhaps have been justified; seamen in their infinite variety of jackets and trousers and hats, their easy attitudes, their dishevelled array of cutlasses and pistols, presented a vast difference from the stiff uniformity of the military. He could be secretly proud of them, all the same. There were no sick men in this party, and the devil-may-care glint in the eyes that watched him from those weather-beaten faces was medicine for his utter weariness. He turned to the Colonel.

'What course for the assault, sir?'

Pawling raised his eyebrows. 'Course? Oh, ah – the direction of attack. There, sir –' he pointed along the outcrop to the left – 'you will perceive a natural ramp leading easily up this cliff. At the top, you are on what we may term the glacis, with two hundred paces or less to go to the foot of the breach.'

As he spoke, his glance flickered uneasily towards the pallid Champerdown. Duncan stepped forward, propping himself with the stick, and raised his powerful voice. The deafening thunder from the guns behind and in front could hardly overtop that voice.

'My lads, we men of *Valiant* have the honour of being the first to meet the Dons face to face. I depend on you to live up to the old ship's name – and to see that the Spaniards never forget it.' He held up his hand quickly, in the nick of time. 'Still! There will be no cheering until the first man is through the breach. —Yes, Mr. Champerdown?'

The young lieutenant was at his elbow, his eyes like saucers in his ashen face.

'S-sir – ' he was trying hard to command his shaking voice – 'the breach, sir – it's barely wide enough for one man at a time, sir! I – I—'

'Thank you, Mr. Champerdown,' said the Flag Captain loudly. 'That is useful knowledge. Post yourself with the second detachment, the starboard watch, if you please.'

Champerdown goggled. 'But, sir—'

'I shall lead the assault myself,' continued Duncan evenly.

Aiding his steps with the stick as inconspicuously as he could, he began to stalk towards the left of the ranks. Colonel Pawling, who at this announcement had stood like a man transfixed, ran after him.

'Confound it, man!' he snarled, with no trace of chilly politeness. 'You can't! You're ill – I can see that!'

'Pray, sir, confine your attention to military matters,' said Captain Duncan without checking his resolute progress.

'But God damn it, sir!' Pawling, completely human now, yelled the words. 'You're unarmed – you've no sword!'

Duncan involuntarily clapped his left hand to his side. It was true. Until now he had not realized that he had left his sword on board *Valiant*. He glanced over his shoulder at the Colonel, smiling faintly.

'I have my stick, sir,' he said.

He had reached the head of the double file. Behind him Pawling was bellowing orders at his aide – double-march, find the trumpeter, sound the Cease Fire. Duncan, grappling with dizziness, thought it wiser not to stop. He gave his brief order as he strode past the petty officers at the head of the files.

'Follow *Valiants*.'

The ledge slanting up the face of the little cliff was broad and easy-angled, but it looked sheerly impossible to Duncan's blurred vision. He willed Keppel's serene features before his mind's eye and heaved himself up it with powerful thrusts from his stick. The cutlass-point of the panting man behind him was wagging about close to his thigh; he must make better speed than this. Habit and tradition, stronger than his more recent hero-worship, brought scraps of prayers and Scripture to his aid. *They shall mount up with wings as eagles....*

He was up. A short slope of shale underfoot, and above, as he raised his eyes, the great mound of debris narrowing at its top to the dark cleft of the breach. A loud continuous crackling, like thorns on a fire but noisier. The air around him full of humming lead. But he was racing up the broken stones of the mound, hardly (it seemed to him) touching them as he was borne upward on legs that were suddenly tireless. A ball from one of the siege batteries crashed into the top of the mound, stinging his face with the flying stone-dust. It was the last shot before the batteries ceased fire, but he neither knew that nor cared. *A bruised reed shall he not break....* Something twitched his hat from his head. Behind him there were hoarse screams and a growing rattle of stones dislodged by falling bodies. Blue shadow closed about him and the broken wall of Fort Moro towered overhead. That wavering blackness with yellow flashes flickering in it must be the breach.

Afterwards, Adam Duncan could humbly thank Providence for a miracle, for it seemed entirely impossible that the Spanish muskets firing through the four-foot cleft of the breach could miss the gigantic captain who came lumbering up the slope at the head of his men, hatless and unarmed. A pistol banged behind his shoulder as he lurched into the ragged gap, deafening him, and a dark figure in front of him fell. The downward sweep of a sword hissed past his nose and struck sparks from the masonry at his elbow. He heard the breathless cheer of *Valiant*'s men merge with the yelling of the Spaniards, saw dimly the levelled barrel of a musket a few inches from his breast, swept up his walking-stick and smote the weapon aside as it exploded. The blow drained the last of his phenomenal energy and overbalanced him at the same time. He pitched sideways and fell to lie with his head and shoulders jammed behind a great block of masonry that had fallen just inside the breach.

He did not feel the trampling of the seamen rushing in across his legs. The din of shots and yells and clashing steel was no louder than the murmur of the sea in his ears, and quickly faded into nothing.

## IV

Captain Duncan heard the murmur of the sea growing louder in his ears, an intermittent surging roar dying in a hiss and a rattle, and then repeating itself. Waves breaking on a shore; he was not on board *Valiant,* then, though his cot was swaying as it sometimes did in a steep sea. He could not at first open his eyes, and when he did it was only the shortest of glimpses between swollen eyelids. Blue twilight and the shoulders of a man close in front against the pale glimmer of stars. He was being borne on a stretcher along a beach – he could hear the scuffing of his bearers' shoes in the sand – and it was evening.

'Halt!'

The rasping voice was familiar. Colonel Pawling was here somewhere. A pause, and then Pawling spoke from farther away.

'You, there! Is that boat from His Majesty's ship *Valiant?* I have dispatches here for your Admiral – also one naval casualty, an officer.'

Whoever was in charge of the boat made some reply inaudible to the man on the stretcher. The Colonel responded incisively.

'Certainly you may ask. Fort Moro is in our hands. The assault led by your naval detachment was completely successful.'

Duncan heard that with a faint thrill of pleasure; but the feeble resurgence of strength that had awakened his senses was fast ebbing. Dimly he knew that he was being lifted at a word of command, heard as from a distance the grunting of the men who lowered his inert body on to the bottom boards. There was a startled exclamation, and then the Colonel's voice again.

'Captain Duncan has the fever. He is unwounded – God only knows why. The damned, bloody fool led the assault – armed with a confounded walking-stick, sir. You may report my words to Commodore Keppel, and –' Pawling cleared his throat noisily – 'and you may add, sir, that I wish we had such another damned, bloody fool in the Army.'

On the last word, Adam Duncan sank contentedly into complete unconsciousness again.

## THREE

### I

'Hands to the braces!'

The faint shout was followed by the muffled drumming of many bare feet overhead. Admiral Duncan, roused from his half-dozing state, lifted his head from the pillow, listening. That had been Cleland, the First Lieutenant, and the order meant either a change of wind or an alteration of course. He frowned to himself in the darkness; and then smiled at his momentary illusion that he was still Captain Duncan of the *Valiant*, whose orders had been that he should be called instantly upon any change of wind or course. That was Fairfax's responsibility now. The Admiral would not interfere with his Flag Captain's working of the ship until it was time for him to command the Fleet in the coming battle. He was in Keppel's place now – Keppel, who had been made an Admiral after that affair at Havana.

His feet were warming up nicely now. Presently he would sleep. There was no shivering, so it was likely that the recurrent fever had quite left him for this time. According to Findlay, Keppel's own surgeon, the fever would have killed him for certain at Havana all those thirty-five years ago had it not been for the superhuman effort he had made in the mad storming of the Fort Moro breach. There, beyond any doubt, was the hand of Providence clearly revealed. . . .

There had been no change in the ship's angle of list, so Cleland had merely been trimming *Venerable*'s sails to a slight change of the wind, which was probably backing a little to the north. If it backed clear round to the west he would have De Winter's ships on a lee shore – assuming he fell in with them. On the other hand, those Dutch ships with their shallow draught could creep close inshore across the miles of shoals off the Lek and leave the deep-hulled British vessels raging impotently out of gunshot. Where would they be when he sighted them? Were they at this minute going about to make for the safety of the Texel again? Or heading to rendezvous at the Channel Isles?

Whichever it was, he reminded himself firmly, Providence had ordained it. He must wait upon the Lord.

To free his mind from useless speculation he thought again of his once beloved Commodore, and with sorrow. For Admiral Keppel had exchanged the sea for politics as soon as *Valiant* paid off on her return from the West Indies in 1764, to Captain Duncan's dismay and utter lack of comprehension. To the big naval captain it seemed incredible that any man – even a chronic invalid like Keppel – should of his own choice exchange a clean life for a dirty one. Duncan himself had no interest whatever in the plots and intrigues of Whig and Tory, relying (like many of his fellow officers) on the permanent officials in Whitehall to prevent the wordy Mohocks in Parliament from interfering with the Navy. But Keppel, a man already unpopular with the Lords of the Admiralty, had chosen to throw in his lot with the Opposition; and his *protégé* and late Flag Captain had suffered because of it.

There was as much of the Stoic as the Presbyterian in Adam Duncan. He did not resent the force of circumstance or complain of misfortunes over which he had no control. But now, looking back from the swaying cot in the darkness of *Venerable*'s cabin, he could see that his association with Keppel had limited his naval career as effectively as had that persistent fever. During the fifteen years of uneasy peace that had followed the end of the Seven Years War the Admiralty had refused all his applications for employment. He had been that pitiable object a sea officer firmly rooted to the shore; a half-pay captain.

Yes, those had been miserable years – all but the last two of them. He remembered the long bouts of illness and the months between them, almost as wretched, when he was well enough to try once more to get a ship, or any sort of active employment, from the chilly gentlemen at the Admiralty. Like the doctors he consulted, they gave him nothing; unlike the doctors, they promised nothing. Those doctors! (The Admiral wagged his head on the pillow, a little sleepily, as he remembered how they had raised his hopes.) Every one of them had a certain cure for his disease and all the cures were different. The waters at Bath, advised one; the springs of Cheltenham are the grand panacea, declared another. There was Doctor Steer and his Opodeldoc, Doctor Bacon and his Cordial Essence of Rhubarb, even –

so desperate had he become – the black-skinned Doctor Mahomet and his novel cure-all called 'Champoo', which involved being rubbed hard all over by the black man's sinewy paws. None of them could stop the regular recurrence of his fever, and it was through no ministrations of theirs that the feebleness left by his long illness after the Havana affair began gradually to leave him. But they had taken his money, nearly all that considerable sum of prize-money that had come to him when *Valiant* paid off. Then he had met Findlay, Keppel's old doctor, in London. Findlay had told him without fuss that there was no cure for his trouble except time, which would slowly lessen its virulence. And he had further said, with the greatest emphasis, that service in the West Indies or on the Mediterranean station would almost certainly kill Captain Duncan.

Then there had been the death of his father the Provost, and the discovery that the little money he had left would barely keep his ageing, querulous mother and the few old servants at Lundie House. Adam Duncan at 36 was a poor man, unskilled in any trade except the one he was unable to practise; a disappointed man, in that the advancement in his naval career which he had hoped for was beyond his grasp; and a lonely man, for he lacked both desire and incentive to acquire the three things considered essential to a gentleman of his position in Society – a strong head for port, a capacity for sexual promiscuity, and a passion for gambling. He had no friends, and in spite of his fine figure and handsome face women found his gentle courtesy dull. For something to do, he had accepted the task of tutoring his widowed sister's children. And, at regular intervals he travelled by coach to London to renew his application for employment.

Hard times indeed for a man who had commanded ships of the line, a sailor who yearned to make the sea his life. More than once (the Admiral recalled with shame) he had cried in his soul, with Job, *What is my strength, that I should wait? And what is mine end, that I should be patient?*

And then had come Henrietta. . . .

The big wrinkled face softened to a smile in the darkness as he thought of Henrietta. He thought of her not as the grey patient woman waiting for his return in the lodging at Yarmouth, but as a lovely girl in a gown of white muslin and cherry ribands, with ringleted brown hair unpowdered. Providence had after all guided him surely, though by devious ways. But for Keppel's politics, but for the Havana fever, he might never have met Henrietta. But for his choice of that particular week in September to go up to London, and the circumstance that all seats on the cheap coach back again had been taken. . . .

At last the Admiral slept.

## II

A chaise and pair was a very infrequent sight in Maundy Place, or indeed anywhere in this northern area of the London slums, though the habitués of the Place might have noticed that this particular chaise – a smart turnout in maroon and yellow – had halted there outside Tom Vinney's house more than once since midsummer. Maundy Place was not a salubrious spot. Ruinous cottages leaned drunkenly against each other, contemplating with their unglazed windows the oblong of bad paving half buried in filth, with a broken stone drinking-trough in the middle. On a bright summer's day the Place was offensive to the nose as well as to the eye, especially if the wind was blowing from the direction of the giant dunghills in Coram's Fields. On a drizzling morning in autumn, if the smell was somewhat less, the scene was a stage nearer the Abomination of Desolation.

The thin drizzle which had driven into shelter the half-naked children who usually played and fought round the stone trough had not prevented a little crowd from collecting in Maundy Place. Half-a-dozen ragged idlers had first arrived to stare at the chaise; a wild-eyed man rather better dressed than the idlers had seized the opportunity to make them a speech; and within five minutes he was standing on the stone trough screeching at a mob of forty or fifty men, most of whom earned a nocturnal – and illegal – living and were therefore at leisure in the forenoon. The orator, having declared himself 'a progressive Whig' (which meant little to his hearers) and 'a friend of the people' (which they understood better), launched into a kind of general commination involving the Tyrant George, Lord North his partner in crime, and the Tory Government as a whole.

The crowd guffawed and shouted bawdy jests, but the speaker had a certain power and displayed, behind his crude vociferations, some knowledge of politics and politicians. The prescriptive right of a London mob to pelt any public speaker was for the moment in abeyance; and one man who bent instinctively to pick up a handful of filth was instantly felled by a backhanded blow from the brawny fellow beside him, who grasped a cudgel in his other hand.

'What care they for liberty?' The orator's voice rose to a howl. 'The liberty they prate of is for themselves – liberty to have their women and their wine, to ride in coaches such as you see yonder –' he flung out a quivering hand towards the chaise – 'liberty to tax and hang and persecute! How have they dealt with our brothers in the American colonies? Sent the redcoats to murder and rape among 'em, because they asked a trifle of liberty! Is this a state to be tolerated by free Britons? Is this—'

He checked in mid career, his glittering eye fixed on a man who had that moment come out of Tom Vinney's house opposite him. Two men, in fact, had emerged, the first being a postboy in shiny boots staggering under the burden of a large wooden case which he bore to the chaise. The other was a stocky gentleman, broad and ruddy of face, whose well-filled breeches were white and creaseless above silk stockings and silver-buckled shoes. This gentleman paused on the steps outside the house to take snuff and raise a shaggy eyebrow at the crowd. Behind him a figure – presumably Mr. Vinney – was briefly visible before the door was swiftly and firmly closed.

'There's one of 'em, by God!' yelled the orator, recovering himself. 'One of the tyrant's myrmidons – one of Fatty North's gang! Ask him what dirty business brings him here, friends of the people! Ask him by what right he and his precious government violate the liberties of trueborn Englishmen—'

He fulminated on. The myrmidon, having swiftly decided that it was best to remove himself from Maundy Place with all speed, had followed nimbly in the wake of his postboy and got into the chaise – pausing a moment, nevertheless, to assure himself that the wooden case had been safely bestowed on the chaise's floor. The pause was his undoing. The mob, as ever, preferred action to speeches; and they had heard just sufficient to persuade them that here was fair excuse for a bit of fun. They turned their jovial attention to the chaise. A shout of 'Down with the bloody Tory!' was followed instantly by 'Down with his bloody chaise!' Flying mud spattered the yellow and maroon paint and a stone shattered the glass above the door panel. The post-boy, who had got his leg over the back of the nearside horse, was pulled down and pitched into the gutter amid roars of laughter. A score of ruffians jostled for places against the offside wheels and high-slung body of the chaise to overturn it, while from the stone trough behind them the orator screeched encouragement to the 'friends of the people'.

The ruddy-faced gentleman, whose big nose the flung stone had missed by a hairsbreadth, clutched the seat of his rocking vehicle and felt acutely anxious. He had no fear for his life or limbs; but the Mob generally removed a victim's breeches or rolled him in the gutter and made off with his wig. The ruddy-faced gentleman's wig and breeches were the best that money could buy.

There was suddenly a very loud shout in a man's deep voice, quite overtopping the uproar outside, and the rocking of the chaise diminished as if some of his tormentors had desisted and turned at the shout. He peered cautiously through the broken window. Looking beyond a narrow sea of heads, he beheld the curious spectacle of the orator – silent now, with goggling eyes and hanging jaw – rising steadily into the air as if drawn heavenward by some invisible rope. It was a second or two before he perceived that the orator was being lifted by the collar in the one-handed grip of a gigantic man wearing a stained boat-cloak.

Adam Duncan, having failed to get a place on the north-bound coach that started from Bateman Street, had been hurrying back to his cheap lodging in the Gray's Inn Road. The morning drizzle had impelled him to don his old boat-cloak over his London clothes, and – unwisely – to attempt a short cut which had brought him to Maundy Place and the fringe of the small but noisy mob that filled it. From his great height he had taken in the situation at a glance: the excited crowd, the man on the trough hounding on his 'friends of the people', the plunging horses and the swaying chaise. He strode forward without hesitation, flinging men left and right and using his quarterdeck voice to advantage.

'Belay that, you fools! Would you harm the horses?'

It was the appeal, as much as the enormous voice, that won him attention. Horses commanded more respect in an Englishman than Members of Parliament. Duncan followed up his momentary advantage without pausing in his stride. He leaped on to the stone trough, seized the orator – a small and scraggy man – by the collar, and held him up at arm's length as though he were a dead rabbit.

'Behold a friend of the people!' he bellowed.

There was a good deal of laughter mingled with the angry shouts that greeted this gesture.

'A friend of spies and Frenchmen, say I!' roared Duncan. 'Take him!'

He swung the unfortunate orator out over the heads of the crowd and let him drop, jumping down instantly himself to force a way towards the chaise. At first no one barred his way. A London mob was always ready to applaud great strength and effective violence, and a good proportion of the crowd was ready at that moment to carry Captain Duncan shoulder-high to Whitehall if he had demanded it. The rest, however, were annoyed at having their legitimate sport interrupted. They surged forward determinedly and were opposed no less determinedly by those who were now resolved to give the chaise free passage. A number of fights began simultaneously. Maundy Place became in a twinkling a muddy battleground of whirling fists and sticks.

Duncan had reached the rearing horses without much opposition. With one hand he gripped the bridle of the nearer beast and with the other plucked to his feet the bruised and filthy postboy.

'Mount and away!' he snapped; and made for the chaise door as the man got his foot into the stirrup.

A knot of struggling men cannoned into him before he could wrench the door open. From inside the chaise came a warning cry of 'Behind you!' He spun round, barely in time to fling up his left arm to ward off the cudgel descending on his head. The blow fell on his hand, and his assailant encountered a right-handed punch that hurled him back on his fellow-rioters. Next moment Duncan was barking his knees on the wooden case inside the chaise, having got through the opened door partly by his own efforts and partly by the efficient hauling of the chaise's occupant. With a trampling of hooves and a grinding of wheels, the vehicle gathered speed and lurched out of Maundy Place by the narrow street at its eastern corner. Wrathful yells and a single stone pursued it; private conflict was now absorbing most of the mob's attention. By the time the ruddy-faced gentleman had assisted his rescuer to sit beside him the din of conflict was gone, its place taken by the creak, rumble, and clatter of the chaise's progress.

'I – thank you, sir,' said Captain Duncan a trifle breathlessly.

'I'm thinking, sir, the boot's on the other foot,' returned his companion; he stood up with some difficulty in the swaying chaise and stuck his head out of the broken window to shout at the postboy. 'De'il take ye, William – rein in! Ye'll have us over!'

He sat down again and the horses slowed from a canter to a trot.

'Believe me, sir, I'm vastly obleeged,' he resumed, turning a pair of very shrewd grey eyes on Duncan. 'I never saw a mob so neatly dealt with, and I've seen mobs a-plenty. This one meant mischief. They'd have overset the chaise with me in it.'

'But little more than that, sir, I fancy.' The Captain pushed his left hand, which was painful, inside the overlap of his waistcoat under his cloak. 'The rogues were out for sport, no more.'

'I dare say you have the right of it. Your London mob have aye a saving touch of humour. Now had it been a pack of Edinbro sawneys they'd no' have stopped till they'd stove in my head. But I'm gey thankful to ye, sir, all the same. At a venture – you're Scottish yourself?'

'I was born in Dundee.'

'A fair city,' nodded the other, 'and a wheen healthier than Auld Reekie. Though mind ye, Dundee has no such plenitude of handsome seats in the vicinity as may be found near Edinbro.'

As he talked, the ruddy-faced gentleman's gaze travelled from his companion's face, where it had noted the pallor and the sunken cheeks to his long legs, which were endeavouring without much success to accommodate themselves round the wooden case that stood against the front panel of the chaise. He gave a dry cough and assumed a slight pomposity of manner which appeared to banish his Scots accent.

'You are no doubt wondering, sir,' he said, 'why a gentleman such as myself should be visiting in Maundy Place.'

'Not at all, sir,' said Duncan shortly and not too tactfully; his hand was hurting abominably with every jolt of the chaise over the ill-laid cobblestones.

'This case is the reason.' The ruddy countenance was a shade redder. 'Two dozen of port, sir, from a cellar that – h'm – is not known to our zealous excisemen. In short, sir, this port has not paid duty.'

'I see.'

Duncan was not sure that he saw, and in any case wine that had paid no duty was common enough at the tables of most English gentlemen. The man beside him seemed relieved.

'Again I'm obleeged, sir, this time for your understanding. You would doubtless support my contention that the lesser gentry should not be privileged above the greater. If Squire Acres may drink his port untaxed, why should not the Lord Advocate?'

Duncan turned quickly. For his class and age, he was unusually ignorant of Parliament and the Cabinet; but he knew one name as that of a clever politician, the brightest of Lord North's henchmen, a 'coming man'.

'The—? Then I've the honour of addressing Mr. Dundas?'

'Henry Dundas, sir, at your service,' smiled the other, with satisfaction. 'And on my side I'm honoured to make the acquaintance of Mr.—?'

'Adam Duncan, sir, captain in His Majesty's Navy. At present,' Duncan added, unable to keep the bitterness from his tone, 'on half-pay.'

He glanced out of the window, not without a touch of anxiety. The chaise was out of the London streets and bowling along a good road between hedges – northward, his seaman's instinct told him. The drizzle had changed to a driving rain.

Mr. Dundas noticed the glance. 'Gad's me life!' he exclaimed. 'Here's me gallivanting on and taking ye willy-nilly. What was your destination, Captain, when ye arrived so providentially in Maundy Place?'

Adam Duncan's reticence was almost pathological, especially on the subject of his broken career. But the Lord Advocate concealed both sympathy and insight behind the bluff Scots exterior he loved to display to the world. From the Captain's brief utterances he was able to discern his whole story – the long frustration of unemployment, the repeated and expensive journeys to London from the North, the vain application for a ship – inevitably vain, as Dundas well knew, from a man politically out of favour. He was shrewd enough to conceal his sympathy; and his comment was practical.

'So ye'd have travelled North tomorrow? Man! I'm near as providential for you as you were for me. Stay by me, and I'll put ye in the way of a seat in a coach that's bound for Scotland two days from now. But – ' he hesitated, tugging at his long upper lip – 'your pardon, Captain, but ye've a man? And baggage?'

Duncan could not conceal embarrassment. He was unable to afford a servant, and his baggage—

'I prefer to travel light, sir,' he muttered. 'I have a small valise slung to my shoulder, beneath this cloak.'

He fumbled one-handed at the fastenings of the cloak. His awkwardness recalled to Mr. Dundas's memory the events in Maundy Place.

'Your left hand is injured,' he said sharply. 'Yon fellow with his damned cudgel – let me see it, sir.'

Reluctantly Duncan extended his left hand. The little finger stuck out at an odd angle from the swelling of an ugly contusion.

'Good God, he broke your finger!' Dundas exclaimed. 'A surgeon – where the de'il will we find a surgeon in this wilderness?'

He half-rose from his seat. Duncan begged him not to distress himself. A surgeon, he pointed out, could do nothing but splint the finger.

'Then we maun splint it as best we can,' said the Lord Advocate; he put his head out of the window and cried to William to stop. 'Ye'll maybe carry a knife?'

The chaise clattered and jingled to a halt. Duncan threw back his cloak (Mr. Dundas noted with secret relief that he was plainly but respectably dressed) and drew a clasp-knife from his breeches pocket. Dundas set to work with it on the wooden case, and in five minutes had produced and trimmed two thick splinters four inches long. With these and the Captain's handkerchief the broken finger was somewhat crudely splinted.

'It will serve,' Dundas said, knitting shaggy brows, 'but

I doubt Rietta would have done it better. She shall attend to you the instant we arrive – she'll enjoy it. And now – ' with a flourish he took a small corkscrew from the pocket of his purple velvet coat – 'we shall broach my Villa de Gaiea. Not a word, Captain. Ye need it, if I don't. Your stoical countenance didna deceive me.'

The cork was drawn, two horn cups produced, and the gentlemen pledged each other in smuggled port. Duncan was glad enough of the wine. He would have liked to suggest a draught for the patient William, huddled in the saddle under the driving rain outside, but William was Dundas's man, not his. The Lord Advocate, who had taken four cupfuls while his companion was drinking one, rammed in the cork, put the bottle back into the case, and shouted to William to drive on.

'We may now expect to endure as far as our destination,' he declared, smacking his lips as the chaise jolted onward. 'Less than two hours to Cheshunt, sir, if this rain hasna turned the road to a morass.'

'Cheshunt, then, is our destination?' Duncan said with a faint smile.

The Lord Advocate thumped a fist on his thigh. 'Gad's me life! I crave your pardon, Captain – you must take me for a kidnapper. But depend upon it, ye'll thank me for the kidnapping when all's done. Here's my plan.'

He launched into a slightly involved tale which was rendered more diffuse by the Villa de Gaiea. Lord Spencer, it seemed, was at present residing at Cheshunt Park, the seat of Lord Russell who was absent abroad. The wife of the Lord Advocate's brother Robert being a connection of Lord Spencer's, and Robert Dundas having business in London, Lord Spencer had invited Robert and his wife and daughter to be his guests at Cheshunt Park during their stay. Henry Dundas was on his way to join this family party for a few days. On the day after tomorrow the ladies were to start back for Scotland in the Dundas coach, attended by servants. If Captain Duncan would accept the hospitality of Cheshunt Park for two nights, he could ride in the coach with them.

Captain Duncan protested. He was a stranger, he was not equipped for genteel society, he was totally unknown to his host. The Lord Advocate waved his protests aside.

'Ye've done me a great service, sir,' he asserted, 'and

that makes ye no stranger to my kin. Brother Robert will say 'twould have done me the world of good to be cudgelled and rolled in the mud, but that's Robert's way. He's President of the Court of Session, ye ken. As for Spencer, he'd walk thirty miles to meet a sea captain. He'll be on to ye about sea power and ship organization, dinna doubt it. If he'd had the sense to throw overboard a wee Whig principle or two, like me, Spencer could have been a Lord of the Admiralty by now.'

These specious arguments held little conviction for Adam Duncan. He saw himself received with concealed dismay, an unexpected and unwanted guest; making polite conversation to the ladies in his broadcloth coat and far-from-new breeches; thrust upon them as a travelling companion for a journey of three days and more. But what could he do? Descend from the chaise and walk a dozen miles back to the Gray's Inn Road through the pouring rain? Request the Lord Advocate to convey him to his lodgings?

Henry Dundas seemed to have divined one of his misgivings.

'And ye'll be a godsend for the journey,' he was saying. 'Robert was sweir to let them go, with only old Fordyce and his blunderbuss against highwaymen and suchlike rogues. He'll loan ye his pistols, Captain, and the ladies will be comfortable instead of anxious. Ye'll be as welcome as flowers in spring.'

There was enough reason in this to outweigh the Captain's doubts. He shrugged his big shoulders imperceptibly, nursing the bandaged hand against the rocking of the chaise.

'The debt will still be on my side, sir,' he said. 'I am honoured to be of any service to your family. I believe,' he added tentatively, 'you mentioned another person. Rietta, if I heard—'

Dundas's gaffaw interrupted him. 'Rietta it was, Captain – Henrietta Dundas, my niece and a braw Scots lassie to boot. 'Tis she will tend that finger of yours. It's not the current fashion for young ladies to meddle with medicine, but Rietta doesna give a damn for the fashion – save in dress, of course.' He wagged his head and chuckled. 'Robert disapproves. Rietta tells him to go read of Scotland's great days, when all Scotswomen had the skill for tending the wounds of their menfolk. Aye, that broken finger will be meat and drink to Rietta.'

Captain Duncan was not sure that this was at all encouraging. But he had resigned himself to the unexpected turn of events and was resolved to take them as they came.

The remainder of the journey in the chaise proved enjoyable despite the gnawing pain of his hand. The Lord Advocate took charge of the conversation and did nine-tenths of the talking, and it was interesting talk. The war with the American colonies; Johnny Burgoyne was collecting an army to teach the colonists what their declaration of independence was worth, but Johnny was no general. An unfortunate business, sir – in confidence, of course. It was to be expected the French would come in, sooner or later. If they did, there'd be no naval captains left on half-pay. Every fighting man would be needed. It could be the start of a long war. . . .

The rain stopped as the chaise splashed and rattled through the hamlet of Waltham Cross. The great trees flanking the drive leading to Cheshunt Park were golden in autumn sunshine.

## III

'There, sir!' said Henrietta Dundas, administering a gentle pat to the sling that hid her complicated bandaging. 'At least you should have less pain now – but I fear, I fear indeed, that it cannot mend properly.'

Her large blue eyes were filled with anxiety as she looked up at Captain Duncan. For her surgery she had made him sit on a chair in the powder-closet adjoining the drawing-room, while she knelt on a cushion beside him. From beyond the half-open door came a babble of conversation in which Henry Dundas's genial tones predominated. Adam Duncan had long ago constructed a screen of manners and graces to conceal his shyness on social occasions; but he was not accustomed to have pretty young women kneeling before him, and dreaded that someone would fling the door wide and make a jest of the scene thus revealed. He stood up hastily, and seizing Miss Dundas's small hand with his massive one hauled her up (as she confided later to her mother) as if she had been an anchor. The handclasp was prolonged by her need to regain her balance. For a moment that became timeless they stood breast to breast, blue eyes held fast by the gaze of astonished grey ones.

The astonishment of that long moment recurred to Captain Duncan many times during the months that followed. Only fifteen minutes had passed since he had first seen Henrietta Dundas among the little group that had come into the hall to welcome Henry. There had been Robert Dundas, tall and saturnine and the very opposite of his ruddy-faced brother; his wife, stout and amiable; and Henrietta – tall and slim in her white muslin and cherry ribands, her high coiffure shining golden in a sunbeam that slanted through the hall window. There had been welcomes and explanations, cries of concern at the story of the rescue and Duncan's injury. With a remarkable display of determination, Henrietta had taken charge of the gigantic stranger – dishevelled as he was, with his stockings muddied and his breeches redolent of Maundy Place – and installed him in the powder-closet while she fetched bandages and poultices. Fifteen minutes, at most – and he had fallen in love. For he realized instantly, though with intense surprise, what had happened to him. He did not suddenly feel that he had known this girl all his life; but he knew that for the rest of his life she must be a part of it.

The Captain became aware that he was still holding Henrietta's hand and staring at her, and that she was blushing furiously. Cursing himself for a clumsy fool, he released the hand and stepped back, trying desperately to think of something to say. The girl spoke first, and rapidly.

'I'm sure Uncle Henry did his best, sir, but he did ill nevertheless. The fracture is a grave one – the bone has quite parted. It should have been set within thirty minutes if it was to mend.' She hesitated. 'There is a bonesetter in the village, an old woman they call a witch—'

'I'll stand by your surgery, ma'am, if you please,' said Duncan, so hurriedly that she smiled.

Henrietta's smile was like sunshine after rain. The Captain found himself smiling back at her, and for some delightful seconds they gazed and smiled in the most ridiculous oblivion of everything except themselves, until Duncan remembered that he had not yet thanked her. She cut short his laboured phrases quickly.

'There is no need for thanks, sir – you rescued my uncle.' She was carefully avoiding his glance. 'The bandage may work loose. It would be as well if I renewed it later today, perhaps after dinner this evening.'

'I shall await the renewing with impatience, ma'am.'

He had intended the words as a mere politeness, but spoke them with low-voiced sincerity despite himself. Henrietta blushed again.

'Where's my surgeon-lassie?' The Lord Advocate stood beaming in the doorway. 'She's no' decided on an amputation, Captain, I trust?'

'The fracture was shockingly botched, Uncle,' Henrietta scolded him. 'You should have driven at once to a surgeon.'

'How was I to know?' Dundas offered his arm. 'There wasna a peep out of the man till we were halfway here.'

Duncan followed them into the drawing-room. Mrs. Dundas, billowy in orange satin, came towards him.

'We have the *whole* story now, Captain,' she said with effusion. 'Believe me, we are *vastly* grateful to you.'

'Though I maintain my expressed opinion,' remarked her husband drily, from behind her, 'that Henry would have derived more benefit from the adventure had Captain Duncan reached the scene ten minutes later.'

'It was *most* fortunate that he reached it at all, Robert,' said Mrs. Dundas severely. 'Now, Captain, I must be your hostess. Spencer is out on one of his walks – he'll return soaked to the skin and muddied to the ears, as usual – so I have ordered your room prepared. It will be ready now. Briggs will assist your toilet.'

She beckoned to a servant in livery who stood by the door.

'Pray remember, sir,' Henrietta said quickly, 'you must not try to use your left hand.'

'I obey you in all things, ma'am,' said Duncan with his best bow; and left her blushing yet again.

He followed the servant to his room with the sensations of one in a dream. It was a state that persisted throughout that day and the next.

There was none of the embarrassment Duncan had feared. Cheshunt Park, despite its noble rooms and army of servants, held an informal party; its tenant was a devotee of field sports and athletics, and disdained the ceremony of Town in the country. The Captain, with the mud cleaned from shoes and breeches and wearing the white silk stockings he fortunately carried in his valise, found himself as presentable as Lord Spencer himself, who dined in a plain russet coat with his red curls imperfectly powdered. Duncan liked him instantly. He was a youngish man, erect and handsome, forthright and direct in all he said and no waster of words. His firm handshake was sufficient to assure the unexpected guest that he was welcome.

At dinner Duncan was dimly conscious that he did not shine as a conversationalist. Henrietta was there in a gown of white satin, her face rosily enchanting below the snowy pile of her evening coiffure and her bare shoulders dazzling in the candlelight. But when the ladies had left them and the port was brought in an enormous decanter, Spencer turned at once to him and began a very pertinent catechism on naval matters, so that the Captain was very soon drawn from the beatific mist that surrounded him. His host had clearly studied the Fleet actions of the Seven Years War, and while his knowledge of ship handling was what might be expected of a landsman who had never set foot in a ship of the line he had a notably quick grasp of detail. Except for such items of news as he had gleaned from the *Gazette*, Captain Duncan was naturally out of touch with naval developments. But he had read the few pamphlets published by the theorists on naval tactics and formed theories of his own. Spencer, roundly denouncing the folly of the British tactics at Bunker Hill, made them the text of a general criticism.

'If we lose the colonies,' he declared, 'it will be by our damned refusal to change our tactics. Our generals won't allow they have anything to learn. It's the same with our admirals.' He turned his lean red face to Duncan. 'You'll not disagree, Captain? The army forms its squares or its ranks and marches bullheaded at the enemy. The navy forms its line of battle and lays itself ship to ship alongside the enemy's line of battle. There's no tactics save those of hammer and tongs.'

'The assumption that one Englishman is the equal of two foreigners seems to warrant the procedure,' observed Robert Dundas with a sour smile.

Spencer ignored him. 'The thing is a tradition, Captain, I know. The whole duty of a sea officer is to close the enemy and batter away with his guns – his courage is in question if he doesn't. But is this the surest way of winning a battle at sea?'

Duncan fingered his glass, frowning. 'I fancy Lord Howe would call you a heretic, my lord. But there are some who have questioned the theory, and to my mind they invite consideration. I had recently a conversation with one John Clerk, a Scotsman who appears to have studied naval tactics—'

'Clerk of Eldin?' interposed Henry Dundas, splashing port into his glass and passing on the decanter. 'A man of parts. I knew him at Edinboro College. Send the bottle round, gentlemen.'

'Mr. Clerk', Duncan went on, 'sees as outmoded the engagement in lines of battle. Or, I had rather say, he perceives the weakness of the tactics.'

'A weakness of both sides in a sea-fight,' Spencer said quickly, his keen eyes on the captain. 'That is, if Clerk perceives a method of making it so.'

'He may have some reason in his theory, my lord. Conceive the line of battle as a fortress. Why batter at it, ship to ship, until it crumbles? Why not a breach in the fortress to begin with?' Duncan leaned forward eagerly. 'Your fleet would be in divisions. Each division would head to break the enemy line before engaging. Much would depend on wind direction—'

'Just so,' Spencer broke in. 'But you would put the enemy into confusion, disturb his plan.' He took a handful of walnuts from a dish and laid them out in two lines on the cloth. 'Now – here's your line of battle. This is the enemy line. There's a fresh breeze blowing from here, by the fruit bowl—'

They spent a happy half-hour, while Robert Dundas watched with his twisted smile and Henry devoted himself to the port, until it was time to join the ladies.

But Adam Duncan was once more enveloped in his rosy mist by the time he climbed into bed. Henrietta had renewed his bandages.

## IV

There was no occasion to use Robert Dundas's borrowed pistols on the long journey northward in the coach. Mrs. Dundas appeared to slumber for most of the time, a faint smile on her placid face. Beside her Henrietta could converse low-voiced with the Captain who sat opposite. It was astonishing how they agreed on every conceivable matter, and how easy it was to tell each other everything they had ever experienced or thought.

A little after Christmas Robert Dundas was engaged in serious argument with his wife.

'The man's penniless, madam. How do they suppose they are to live?'

'You exaggerate, Robert, as always,' returned his wife comfortably. 'He has sufficient for them to live quietly, as they intend. Besides, there is Henrietta's dowry. And you know well that Nellfield is without a tenant.'

About the same time, Henrietta Dundas was in conference with her uncle.

'Papa does listen to you, Uncle Henry,' she was saying, 'though he pretends not to. Do, do intercede with him for us. Will you?'

'If my bonny Rietta can't twist brother Robert round her finger, how shall I succeed?' The Lord Advocate pulled her on to his knee. 'Forbye, my fee for intercession might be a heavy one.'

Henrietta disengaged herself quickly; when he was well filled with port, as now, Uncle Henry was inclined to fondle in an unseemly manner.

'But will you – please?' she demanded again.

Henry Dundas, suddenly serious, tugged at his upper lip. His shrewd glance dwelt on her a moment and then went past her into vacancy; or perhaps into the future.

'I'll do so, Rietta,' he said slowly, 'on one condition. That ye'll promise me never to influence Adam Duncan, directly or indirectly, towards giving up his profession.'

The girl frowned. 'But why, Uncle?'

Dundas hesitated. It was his way to be thrifty in small things and it had paid him before now. Rietta's big seaman might just possibly be useful.

'I have my ambitions, lass,' he said offhandedly. 'It's like enough I'll realize them with the coming war to jink me up. Then I'll have need – and so will England – of admirals who care more for their service than for politics. Men like your Adam Duncan. That's why.'

'I promise,' said Henrietta quickly, and bent to kiss him.

So Captain and Mrs. Duncan, who were married in the spring of 1777, resided at Nellfield near Edinburgh in great content. Their happiness remained undisturbed for more than a year, until the Continental powers made their expected gesture in support of the American colonies. Captain Duncan was duly recalled to service, and by December 1778 was in command of His Majesty's ship *Monarch*, 74 guns. In this, as in the circumstances of his first meeting with Henrietta, he very naturally perceived the orderly arrangements of Providence.

# FOUR

## I

'Sir! If you please – sir!'

Admiral Duncan became aware of a scratching or nibbling at his left shoulder. He stirred and grunted, thinking vaguely of rats; it could have been a rat – there were plenty aboard *Venerable*. But there had been a voice. It came again, with another tentative scratching at his shoulder.

'Sir – two bells of the morning watch, sir. Struck two minutes ago.'

The Admiral sat up, slowly and with a groan. In the darkness he could just discern a small, slight figure beside his cot. He shook his big head to banish the fumes of sleep and growled a question.

'Who is that?'

'Stewart, sir. You gave orders to be called at two bells, sir.' The voice was treble, and nervous. 'I – I couldn't make you hear, sir. I didn't like to – to shake you.'

Stewart was the most junior of the midshipmen, Duncan remembered. He had joined at Yarmouth only four days ago.

'I was to be called at two bells, Mr. Stewart,' he said in his deep voice, kindly enough. 'Always obey orders to the letter, my boy, even if it means shaking an Admiral.'

'Yes – I mean aye aye, sir,' stammered the boy.

'Very well, Mr. Stewart.'

As the cabin door closed behind the midshipman the Admiral swung his legs over the side of the cot. Already his senses had told him that *Venerable* was still on the starboard tack with a fresh northerly wind and a moderate sea. A rhythmic clanking from somewhere underfoot meant that Fairfax had the pumps going. He must remember to see that those pumps kept at work right up to the moment of engagement; no one knew better than the Admiral just how ancient were *Venerable*'s timbers and how much it was to be feared that she would actually founder from her own leakiness during a battle. She was the oldest 74 in the Navy and ought to have gone to the shipbreakers long ago, as he had repeatedly represented to the Admiralty. The point was emphasized when he padded stiffly across to turn up the wick of the oil-lamp and splashed with his bare feet in the puddle of water that swilled against the bulkhead. Evidently it was raining. No amount of caulking seemed to stop that leak in the deck overhead, and he had had his cot moved from there for that reason.

In pulling on his breeches he caught his ring in the lining and took a second or two to free it; it was the double ring that linked the third and fourth fingers of his left hand – Henrietta's idea, that had been, to counteract the weakness of the broken finger that had never mended. He was reminded that he had been thinking of Henrietta when he dropped off to sleep, and smiled to himself. How she would have scolded him for putting on his stockings over wet feet! It would be characteristic of her to worry more over that little incident of the immediate present than over the possibility of his being killed or mutilated in the near but uncertain future. At this hour, six in the morning of October 10th (which would be October 11th by landsman's reckoning) she would certainly be fast asleep in her bed at the Yarmouth lodging.

The swirling puddle flowed over his buckled shoes while he was taking his tarpaulin from its hook. It was the sign-manual, that puddle, of twenty years of slow but relentless descent from fine ships to the most decrepit vessel of all his career. *Monarch* had been a fine ship – she was with him now, carrying his Vice-Admiral – and in her he had taken his full share of the battle off Cadiz, engaging three Spanish line-of-battle ships, one of which, the *San Augustin,* had struck to him. It was in accordance with his persistent ill-fortune that the seas should have been so heavy that it was impossible to launch a boat to take possession, so that she won clear away into Cadiz. And then *Monarch* had been ordered to the West Indies station. His doctors had declared it certain death for him to go with her; his recurrent fever would see to that. Henrietta's pleading had turned the scale and he had resigned his command. They had given him the *Blenheim,* 90, and after that indecisive action off Cape Spartel she too had been ordered to the West Indies. Again he had had to resign his command. It was natural enough that he should have ended as captain of the Portsmouth guardship *Edgar* after those two resignations. They had duly made him a Rear-Admiral – at fifty-six. But he fancied his naval career might have finished there, had it not been for the new war with France and the urgent need of fighting-men to combat the growing threat of the Revolutionary power on every coast of Europe.

Menzies entered the cabin. The Admiral absently bade him good-morning and went out past the clash and slap of the marine sentry's salute into the draughty alleyway at the foot of the companion.

It could even be that he owed his promotion to Vice-Admiral, and his command of the North Sea Fleet, to nothing more than his connection with members of the war-time Government. Henrietta's Uncle Henry was not only Secretary for War and Treasurer of the Navy but the friend and adviser of the Prime Minister. Duncan's own friend and old acquaintance, Earl Spencer, was First Lord of the Admiralty. The suspicion that they might of their kindness have given him this, the least coveted command in the Navy, depressed him. But only for a moment. Up the wet wooden steps of the ladder he came, to emerge on deck into a fresh wind laden with mingled rain and spray, and his depression was instantly blown away.

The huge masts and bellying canvas of the flagship leaned overhead against a scurry of clouds still dark with the fading night. Under all plain sail *Venerable* was ploughing across a lumpy grey-green sea, with no horizon visible through the dark grey curtains of mist and rain-squall. As Duncan set foot on the quarterdeck Fairfax came across from the weather rail, where he had been chatting with Clay the second lieutenant.

' 'Morning, sir,' said Fairfax, touching his cocked hat, which was set very squarely on his big head.

His stocky figure looked stockier still in tarpaulin jacket and high leather seaboots. He could have remarked upon the course or the wind, or inquired if the Admiral had slept well; but the Flag Captain was a man of few words, which suited Duncan perfectly.

'Good morning, Captain. You have a position?'

'By dead reckoning, sir. Twenty-one leagues east-nor'-east of Yarmouth.'

'Thank you, Captain.'

Leaning against the wind and the slant of the deck, the Admiral went towards the rail above the helm and peered down at the duty quartermaster juggling endlessly with the spoke-handles of the wheel. The binnacle light still burned, though there was now just enough grey daylight to show the compass dial. North east by north. Ye so. That was probably sufficient allowance for *Venerable*'s leeway with this wind. And if the wind held fair, his ships should be off the Texel by early afternoon. He would send in his fastest frigate – *Circe*, if they fell in with her – to find out whether De Winter's ships were still at sea or back again at their safe anchorage.

As he had expected, his inspection of the compass had enabled Fairfax and Clay to move unhurriedly to the lee rail, leaving the weather side of the quarterdeck free for him to walk. Duncan always felt a little mean in depriving Fairfax of a captain's privilege, especially as he himself had a stern gallery for his pacing, but he loved his morning walk by the uptilted weather rail too much to relinquish it. He would not interrupt it now until Menzies summoned him to breakfast – not even to go below and put on his seaboots. With his big hands clasped behind him and the thin rain setting his tarpaulin coat a-glisten, he began his slow fore-and-aft pacing.

At his first turn aft he caught a glimpse of two ships on *Venerable*'s larboard quarter, half seen through a grey squall – *Isis* and *Belliqueux*, at a guess. His ships on this station had been changed so often that he had difficulty in identifying them by their rig. Except that he was always given the oldest and least seaworthy ships in commission he had never known what to expect. A ghostly hull looming not far away on the starboard quarter was probably the old *Monarch;* Onslow, his second-in-command, would lead a division and was no doubt making a point of keeping in touch with his senior. The other seven ships of his present fleet were, he hoped, just beyond the encircling walls of mist and rain. *Russell* and *Adamant* were already cruising off the Dutch coast, where they had been left with the frigate *Circe* to maintain the blockade; with luck, three more ships of the line might join him before he engaged De Winter's fleet. He would have a battle-line of sixteen then, against De Winter's possible twenty – sixteen old and unweatherly vessels against a fleet of well-found ships that had had two years in which to refit and make good every conceivable defect. In the important matter of knowledge of Dutch waters, however, he could count himself the Dutch admiral's equal. Duncan's big weatherbeaten face crinkled in a wry smile as he tried to recall how many times he had smelled his way along those big shoals from Vlieland to the Lek and back again, to and fro month after month for two long hard years, more often than not battling desperately with the westerlies that tried relentlessly to send his ships aground on that terribly dangerous lee shore. Two frustrating years, for he had hoped vainly for the emergence of the Dutch Fleet from that narrow gut they called the Texel, between Texel Island and the Helder on the mainland of North Holland. To have kept them bottled up there so long was no doubt of great advantage to England, threatened as she was by invasion; but it was small satisfaction, and it had meant the most severe hardship for men and vessels alike. Someone in the Government had taken pity on a Vice-Admiral of sixty-four years perpetually at sea in the winter gales. The First Lord of the Admiralty had known better than to agree when it was suggested that a comfortable seat on the Board of Admiralty would suit an old man better than the quarterdeck of a leaky flagship. Duncan had been sent a copy of his reply and still treasured it with secret pride; indeed, he had its pungent sentences by heart. *The services of Admiral Duncan are so valuable in the situation in which he now acts that he could not possibly be spared from it without detriment to the service* – Spencer was clever enough to be aware that the only man who could manoeuvre a fleet against De Winter, if he ever came out into his own shallow and tempestuous waters, was Adam Duncan. That was why, a year later, he had been entrusted with the command of Uncle Henry's mad expedition.

The Admiral's smile changed to a grin as he recalled Henry Dundas's insanity; it was, he reflected, a common insanity of clever politicians. For Mr. Dundas, now able to call himself Right Honourable and 'one of His Majesty's Principal Secretaries of State', had suddenly conceived himself a military genius. A punishing blow at revolutionary Holland was sorely needed, if only – as he himself put it naively – 'to give a good impression of the war in England'. It could be given, and this wasteful blockade of the Texel ended, at one single brilliant thrust. Since the forts at the Texel mouth prevented British ships from entering, the forts must be captured. Forts were military objectives, so soldiers would be landed to capture them. Doubtless a simple and obvious solution to the civilian mind—

'Your breakfast is sairved, sir.'

Menzies was beside him, screwing up his gaunt face against the rain. The Admiral turned, acknowledged the watchful Fairfax's salute, and followed his steward below.

'Coffee, sir,' croaked Menzies. 'Bread baked two days syne. Broiled Yarmouth herrings.'

The Admiral sat down with a good appetite. It was the one advantage of leaky ships that the ship's company got fresh food each time they had to put in for repairs; and he was partial to broiled herrings. It was satisfactory to think that the hands would be having the same food as their Admiral, except for small beer instead of coffee. He had been finishing a broiled herring, he remembered, when Captain Drury had come on board from Yarmouth. There would have been little enjoyment in that herring if he had read Drury's dispatches before starting on it. . . .

## II

'William O'Bryen Drury, post captain, at your service, sir.' Captain Drury introduced himself with immense satisfaction. 'My apologies for boarding you so early, but my business is urgent.'

He was a smallish, plumpish man with a round red face and an eager manner. Duncan knew of him as a sea officer of some repute, at present without a ship despite his very influential connections; the Admiral's flag captain had expressed the opinion that Drury was one of those Whitehall meddlers.

'Pray excuse the state of my cabin, sir,' said the Admiral politely. 'I have but just breakfasted.'

'I'm a trifle dishevelled myself, I fear, sir,' Drury said. 'I've come post from London, driving through the night.'

His manner implied reproach of those who slept while he so drove. The Admiral was instantly sympathetic.

'Then you've not breakfasted? That must be remedied.'

He raised a finger to the steward who was bearing out the remains of his meal.

'No, I thank you,' said the captain hastily. 'I – ah – took a refection while I waited for a boat to be found.'

'Then be seated, Captain, and let us hear your business.'

Captain Drury drew up a chair and sat down in one swift motion. He drew a sealed packet from his breast and held it out with a dramatic gesture.

'From the First Lord, sir,' he said weightily. 'Most urgent – and secret,' he added, darting a suspicious glance at the cabin door, which was on the point of closing behind the steward.

Duncan broke the seal. He was frowning as he unfolded the stiff paper; already he could guess what he was to read. The letter was headed 'Admiralty: September 30, 1796' and signed by Spencer. Yes, it was as he had thought. Incredibly, Government was proposing to implement that insane scheme of Uncle Henry's. *'I send you this by Captain Drury, to whom we have given an acting order for the standard. He will explain to you at large all that has passed here relative to the proposed plan . . . carried into execution . . . ensure its success. . . .'* There was no doubt of it. In spite of what he had written to Spencer the moment he had heard of the scheme, in spite of his reasoned arguments against it, the irrefutable facts of season and wind and soundings, the First Lord was backing the plan. *'Captain Drury, whose zeal and spirit upon this occasion do him infinite credit'* – that was a veiled reprimand for Duncan's lack of spirit, no doubt – *'has thrown out a hint which I therefore think it right to mention to you, that, as he has planned this undertaking, he may be employed to execute it. . . .'*

So Drury had worked out the details of Uncle Henry's scheme for him. Drury was to explain those details to the Admiral, and Drury was to organize and command the landing operations. Naturally, Drury would receive the credit for what, if it succeeded, would be a brilliant and very valuable success. In the Admiral's considered opinion the chances of success in summer, with an easterly breeze, were fifty to one against; in the present season of westerly gales, a thousand to one against.

*'I write in haste,'* Spencer ended his letter, *'as Drury wishes to set off as soon as possible.'*

By the time the Admiral had read the letter twice the impatient Drury had risen from his chair with a muttered excuse and was pacing restlessly about the cabin. Duncan bade him sit down again, using a curtness unusual with him. Perceiving at once that it was unfair to vent on the captain an irritability which Spencer and Dundas had roused, he proceeded more gently and with marked courtesy.

'Earl Spencer speaks very highly of your plan, sir. I understand I am to hear its details from you. If you will be so good—'

'Certainly, sir.' Captain Drury was all eagerness. 'You know in outline what is proposed. The objective, of course, is to destroy the Dutch Fleet in its anchorage. My plan is perfectly simple, and for that reason is unlikely to fail. In the first place, a sufficient force of military—'

The captain's small dark eyes sparkled with enthusiasm as the words flowed from him. He was clearly a first-rate organizer and had an excellent memory; it was evident that he had taken pains to discover the needs of a large body of soldiers landed on an enemy shore, and he had forgotten nothing. Every detail – the number and size of boats required, the oiled skin covers for the locks of the muskets, the rockets for signalling the capture of the forts – was ready on the tip of his tongue. Admiral Duncan's little fleet of six vessels was to be augmented by four ships of the line from Portsmouth; these were already waiting to receive on board the 10th and 87th regiments of infantry under the command of Colonel Doyle. Two fireships, the *Incendiary* and the *Megaera,* would join the squadron, to be used against the anchored Dutch vessels as soon as the English ships began the passage of the Texel. Secrecy, explained Captain Drury, was desirable, though not perfectly essential, for the success of his plan, so the troops would be landed in darkness or in thick weather. One regiment would be landed on the northern jut of the mainland that formed one post, as it were, of the Texel's narrow gateway, to storm and take the Helder fortress. The other would land on the Texel island itself to capture the fort on the north side of the entrance. Immediately on receiving the signal that both forts had been taken, Admiral Duncan would lead his fleet in through the entrance and destroy the Dutch ships at anchor inside. If practicable – 'and I am confident it will be,' averred the captain – the military would then take possession of the Texel island and the Helder peninsula.

The Admiral listened without interruption to this exposition, his big hands folded in his lap and his grey eyes steady on the voluble captain. When Drury had finished, throwing himself back in his chair with an air of triumph, there was a pause, for the Admiral continued to sit immobile and reflective, in silence. Captain Drury shifted restlessly and sat up straight.

'You discern some flaw, sir?' he demanded incredulously.

'No.' The Admiral shook his head slowly. 'Your plan is flawless, sir. I congratulate you upon it.'

Drury leaned forward with a smile. 'Thank you, Then—'

'The flaw,' Duncan went on gently, as a father instructing his son, 'occurs before your plan begins. You speak of landing the troops in boats. You have never, I fancy, cruised off this part of the Dutch coast, Captain?'

'No, sir. But I have experience of similar coasts, not to mention military landings—'

'Then you will be unaware of its peculiarities. Along the part we are dealing with there is shoal water for several miles out from shore. It faces east and the prevailing winds are westerlies, at this season normally of gale force, which throw up a barrier of surf through which no ship's boat could hope to pass. It follows that except in a rare condition of calm or an easterly breeze my ships can neither come in close enough to send away boats nor be assured that a single boat will reach the shore.'

Captain Drury, at first disconcerted, had quickly recovered himself. Earl Spencer had warned him to expect this opposition.

'I assure you, sir,' he said emphatically, 'I have considered all this and planned accordingly. For the shoal water, I have the *Redoubt* – the floating battery from the western squadron – which has a very shallow draught. I shall transfer both regiments on board her so soon as we are off the Dutch coast, and the landings will be made from her.'

'Twelve hundred men,' murmured the Admiral as though to himself. 'All their food and equipment. A great number of boats as deck cargo. An onshore wind and a heavy sea.'

The captain pretended not to hear him. 'As for the westerlies – surely, sir, these do not blow ad infinitum. I naturally intend to wait for a favourable opportunity, whether a change of wind or a dead calm.'

'I see,' Duncan nodded. 'From my own experience, Captain, I venture to predict a very long wait. – But I must apologise.' Drury nodded and looked expectant. 'There is, after all, a flaw in the plan you so clearly laid before me.' Drury's face showed impatience and disbelief. 'The entrance past the Texel is so narrow that it admits of but one line-of-battle ship passing through at a time, and that with a fair wind. And it runs east and west.'

'I don't understand you, sir,' complained the captain irritably as he paused.

Duncan raised his shaggy brows. 'No? But an easterly wind, sir, blowing offshore – while it might enable the landings to take place – would make it totally impossible for me to take my ships in through the Texel gut.'

Drury stared and swallowed hard. But he was disconcerted for a moment only.

'In that case, sir,' he said hardily, 'I would await a wind from north or south.'

'You'll need patience, then, Captain. You and Colonel Doyle and two regiments of infantry. A week, a fortnight, three weeks of beating to and fro—'

The captain jumped to his feet, very stiff and very red in the face. 'I believe you make difficulties, Admiral Duncan!' he snapped, sticking out his chin.

'You may believe the difficulties are there, Captain Drury,' Duncan said mildly. 'It was not I that made them.'

'You decline to accept my plan?'

'I have already given the First Lord my opinion that any such plan – not merely yours, sir – is rash and very unlikely to succeed. I am, of course, at his orders.'

Drury snatched up his cocked hat from the table where he had laid it. 'Very good, sir! I'm to take that answer to Earl Spencer?'

'In a moment, sir, in a moment.' The Admiral rose ponderously and a trifle wearily to his feet. 'My senior officers are waiting to offer you the hospitality of the wardroom. At your convenience thereafter, you will oblige me by carrying my letter to the First Lord.' His lips twitched almost imperceptibly. 'It will of course be most urgent – and secret.'

Captain Drury darted a malignant glance at him. 'Aye aye, sir,' he said curtly, and departed.

The Admiral took pen and ink and paper from an escritoire and sat down to write.

*'My dear Lord, – Further to my letters of August 30, September 10, and September 22, on this subject. . . .'*

### III

To the letter, carried by Captain Drury the First Lord replied at once, stiffly and with biting sarcasm.

*'Admiralty: October 3, 1796*

*'Dear Sir, – When any enterprise promising considerable advantage is undertaken, more especially in the military line, it is quite impossible that some risk should not be the necessary attendant upon it. . . . I think it is hardly fair to suppose that because we are not quite sure of fine weather there must be blowing weather, nor because we cannot bring the successful event of the attempt to a mathematical demonstration that we should despair so much as not even to take the chance of trying it. . . .'* And more to the same effect, ending on a slightly ominous note: *'I should be glad to have another line from you by return of post, and to know when you think you will be ready to put to sea.—Yours &c., SPENCER.'*

Admiral Duncan seemed to see the impatient shade of Captain Drury at the First Lord's elbow, with Mr. Dundas hovering in the background. It was easier still to perceive the contrast between Captain Drury's 'zeal and spirit' and his own craven hanging-back as it must appear to those at the Admiralty. He did not allow himself to be moved by these considerations. He knew, beyond any knowledge that Spencer or Dundas or Drury could possibly possess, that the plan was an ill-advised and reckless scheme with minimal prospect of success, and he would continue to say so until he received a direct order to sail with the expedition. Uncle Henry could value his design for the 'good impression of the war in England' it would give; Duncan would not approve it though the impression given by his disapproval might ruin his career and brand him coward. He set his jaw and wrote again to Spencer. The reply from the First Lord was prompt and brief.

*'Private. Admiralty: October 5, 1796*
*'Dear Sir, – I have not time today (being the first day of the session of Parliament) to do more than acknowledge the receipt of your letter. . . . I have seen Captain Drury this morning and have talked it over with him again . . . you will, of course, before you sail, have full instructions and communications from us on every part of the business. . . . Yours &c., SPENCER.'*

The die was cast and he would have to conform to its mould. At this moment His Majesty's commands, which for fifty years he had been bound to obey without question, must be in preparation. With a sense of relief (for it was curiously easy to exchange moral for physical courage) Duncan threw all his energies into preparing his squadron for sea. Firmly he dismissed all his doubts, quelling them when they returned by fixing his mind on the consequences of a successful enterprise. These could be valuable to his country. Lord Malmesbury, as he knew from Spencer, was being sent to Paris to attempt to negotiate a peace with the Jacobin revolutionaries. It was an attempt already doomed to failure, in Duncan's opinion; but there could be no doubt that Malmesbury's hand would be enormously strengthened if he held the cards of a Dutch Fleet destroyed and enemy territory occupied by British troops.

The October gales had arrived. A letter from Spencer dated October 8 began: *'It blows so fresh now that I am very glad you are still in Yarmouth Roads.'* The Admiral smiled grimly as he read the words; Spencer's common sense was stirring and unsettling his rash confidence. But the Plan was adding to itself. Two captured Dutch fishing-vessels, the First Lord continued, were to be converted into fireships to assist *Incendiary* and *Megaera,* and 'a very clever and intelligent artillery officer' named Mr. Bell would be sent to assist in the conversion. To preserve secrecy as to their purpose, it was to be pretended that the squadron was escorting these non-combatants back to their native shores. A blockade of Amsterdam was to be declared immediately the Texel fleet was destroyed.

The storms of the equinox blew on, lashing the Channel coasts and the dreary shores of the North Sea. On October 14th the expected package of documents reached Admiral Duncan: orders for the Admiral from the Commissions for executing the Office of Lord High Admiral of Great Britain and Ireland, issued by 'His Majesty's design' and at 'His Majesty's pleasure'; copies of the orders for Colonel Doyle in command of the soldiery, signed by Henry Dundas at Parliament Street; a friendly covering letter from Evan Nepean, the Admiralty secretary. Three days later came an impatient letter from Spencer – 'I hope that this will only reach you at sea' – but at Portsmouth the weather had been so rough that the two regiments had been unable to embark until that day. In thick and squally weather the rendezvous was made without mishap. On October 21st Admiral Duncan's squadron – battleships, fireships, floating battery, three frigates, two regiments of infantry and a detachment of artillery – was off the Texel.

## IV

'*Ramillies* is signalling, sir!' shouted Captain Gregory above the screech of the wind in the flagship's shrouds; he turned, dodging a cascade of spray. 'Where the devil's the signal midshipman?'

'Here, sir!'

Midshipman Larkin's usually piercing voice was almost lost in the uproar of gale and sea. The Admiral, an elephantine figure in his tarpaulins, staggered up the tilted wet planks of the quarterdeck to get nearer to him. Larkin was bravely dragging himself up by the mizzen shrouds to stand on the rail, so that he could see above the haze that hung on the leaping wave-tops. He hung on with one hand and tried to steady his glass with the other, while drifts of spray blew past his thin legs.

'*Venerable*'s pendant, sir – "am sending boat".'

He sprang down, and at the Admiral's nod reeled away to get the acknowledging pendant from the signal locker. Duncan remained at the weather rail, steadying himself with a hand on the smooth wet wood. He was hatless, as he always preferred to be when the excuse offered, and his white hair tugged and fluttered in the wind. A silver stubble, glistening in the grey light, covered his heavy jowls; in the plunging, lurching *Venerable* it had been impossible to use a razor for three days, even when – as now – she was hove-to under reefed topsails.

'Someone's in a hurry, sir.' The flag captain had come up beside him. 'It's moderating fast. In another hour he'd have had a drier passage.'

'Yes,' said Duncan briefly.

*Ramillies*' boat was certainly bringing Colonel Doyle on board and probably Captain Drury as well. It was annoying to have to receive the military commander looking like a vagabond, when an hour or so later he would have had a shave – but it was likely enough that Doyle too had had no chance to use his razors. If Doyle had shaved three times in the past fourteen days, Duncan reflected, he had been lucky.

'The wind is certainly moderating,' he said to Gregory with the faintest hint of emphasis.

Gregory took the hint. In a moment he was roaring at his first lieutenant, the shout was echoed on the main deck, and the topmen were racing like monkeys up the windswept shrouds and out along the topsail yards. To shake the reef out of the topsails as soon as the gale let them was a sensible precaution; on this lee shore they were endlessly clawing off in the teeth of the gales. Duncan glanced up at the flapping canvas, where the men's heads showed as black dots against the flying clouds. That was a new mizzen topsail, for the other had blown to shreds a week ago in a vicious squall off Nordwyck. He lowered his glance to the tossing expanse of grey waves, each with its scudding crest of yellowish white. Beyond, through the brume of the spindrift, he could see the bulky loom of *Ramillies* and the shadowy forms of three other ships farther away to windward. *Redoubt* was not among them. The Admiral made a wry mouth as he thought of the state of those on board the unweatherly floating battery after a fortnight of continual heavy seas and adverse winds; and the soldiers in the other ships would be in little better case. Twelve hundred landsmen in red coats, packed like sardines in the stinking 'tween-decks—

'Masthead reports *Montagu* and *Eurus* in sight to larboard, sir,' said Gregory, fetching up at his side with a lurch.

That made seven of them, then. Forty-eight hours ago he had been able to account for all his squadron except the two converted Dutch fireships, which had not been sighted since the gale on the fifth day. It was something of a feat to have kept so many of his heterogeneous collection together, after fourteen days – fourteen days of beating about, to and fro, up and down the North Holland coast in the foulest of late autumn weather and with a relentless onshore wind. Twice they had seen the coast clearly. The second time – it had been on the 30th – Colonel Doyle had had himself rowed across to the flagship during a lull. He was informed the coast of the Helder was in sight, he told the Admiral acidly; he believed it was their objective. What was the purpose to be served in delaying the landing? Duncan had taken the Colonel, somewhat against his will, up to *Venerable*'s maintop, and lent him his telescope. Even from that height the miles of boiling surf were visible and plainly impassable. Colonel Doyle had departed convinced but leaving the impression that he held Admiral Duncan responsible for the continued bad weather.

A black fleck appearing and disappearing on the waves halfway between *Ramillies* and the flagship caught Duncan's eye.

'Have the sideboys ready to pipe the military commander on board, if you please, Captain,' he said.

'Aye aye, sir.'

The flag captain went to the taffrail to give the order. Duncan watched the boat come nearer, soaring and diving out of sight behind the crests. Soon he could see two cloaked figures huddled in the sternsheets, one bigger than the other. Doyle and Drury, then. If they thought to persuade him to go in any nearer to the Texel they must be mad. Gregory was having a ladder rigged over the lee side amidships; Doyle could hardly expect the gangway lowered for him in this weather. There were sea officers who would have enjoyed watching an army colonel make that hazardous leap from a tossing boat to a dangling ladder. Duncan stayed by the weather rail while the boat rocked past *Venerable*'s stern and vanished from sight under the lee of her hull. When the squealing of the pipes announced that the visitors had come safely over the side he turned and descended the ten steps of the quarterdeck ladder to receive them.

Colonel Doyle was a big man, nearly as tall as the Admiral and twenty years his junior. His angular face (noticeably unshaven, Duncan was relieved to see) wore an expression of mingled worry and bitterness and was comically streaked by the damp powder that had run down it from his hair. It was evident that Captain Drury, who stood uncertainly at the colonel's shoulder, had even yet not found his sea-legs after so long a stay in Whitehall. Both officers replied with the briefest of ceremony to Duncan's greeting and were at once ushered by the Admiral to his cabin.

'Pray don't think I'm inhospitable, gentlemen,' said Duncan when he had seated them and sent the steward for glasses and a bottle of Madeira, 'but your boat will have to lie off to await you. In this weather seamen should not be asked to remain in an open boat for too long.'

'Our business won't detain them long, sir,' growled the Colonel.

He threw back his cloak, revealing the scarlet jacket beneath it and the dark patches where seawater had soaked the cloth. Seated beside him, Drury seemed fascinated by the big chandelier (now converted for oil lighting) which depended from the deckhead above the table. With each heavy roll of the ship the chandelier swung steadily across in a great arc, and the captain's bloodshot eyes followed it.

'First, sir,' Doyle said abruptly, 'is there any sign of this cursed weather leaving this cursed coast?'

'A shift of wind will be the first sign, Colonel. Of that there is presently no sign at all.'

'If it should shift, would there be an opportunity – any hope at all – of making an effective landing?'

Duncan glanced curiously at him. This was the first time the colonel had sought his opinion.

'Not unless the break was a long one, two or three days of fair weather at least,' he replied. 'Sea and surf must have time to subside before the boats can go in.'

The steward brought the wine and went out. Duncan filled the three glasses. Drury seized his instantly and drained it at a gulp.

'And what, sir, are the chances of this two or three days' break?' demanded Doyle, who had left his own wine untasted.

Duncan shrugged his big shoulders. 'I can only say that they are very small, Colonel. It is the fourth day of November. Winter weather is to be expected. Yet if we wait another week there is the bare possibility—'

'That suffices, sir,' grated the colonel; he snatched up his wineglass and tossed the Madeira down his throat. 'Admiral Duncan, I'm here to submit that this expedition should return to England forthwith.'

The Admiral's shaggy brows lifted high and his eyes opened very wide; he had not expected this. Colonel Doyle, having crossed his Rubicon, hurried on, giving the table an occasional thump with his fist as if to goad himself.

'A good half of my men are too sick to stand. The rest couldn't aim a musket if they were landed tomorrow. This cursed pitch and toss, up and down, shaking and swinging—'

Captain Drury suddenly rose, and with a piteous look at the Admiral staggered out of the cabin holding his hands over his mouth. Duncan stooped to pick up the small silver bell that had fallen from the table and was rolling about the deck.

'Find Captain Drury and take him some brandy,' he instructed the steward who entered at his ring.

'Sixteen days since we sailed from Yarmouth Roads.' The colonel was growling on in complete disregard of Drury's exit. 'Sixteen days, in conditions I wouldn't keep a dog in. Small wonder, sir, the men are incapacitated. Had they been landed immediately we arrived off the Texel, according to plan, I'll stand to it they'd have given a good account of themselves.'

He glared resentfully at the Admiral. Duncan met the glare steadily.

'You suggest, Colonel,' he said in mild interrogation, 'that I am to blame both for their accommodation and for not landing them according to plan?'

Colonel Doyle swallowed. 'I do not say so, sir.'

'Nor, I trust, do you intend to say so in your report?'

'Good God, sir, I'm not a backguard!' Doyle flared. 'I blame no one. As for the proposal to withdraw – I've as yet no answer from you on that point – I take full responsibility.'

'And Captain Drury?' Duncan said softly. 'He originated the plan, did he not?'

'Drury was the first to suggest withdrawal,' said the colonel frigidly. 'And now, sir, I again request your answer. Again, with respect, I submit that this expedition should sail for England at once.'

Duncan rose to his feet and walked to the stern windows.

For a few seconds he stood there silent, swaying easily to the rolling of the ship and gazing unseeingly at the salt-caked panes. Then he swung on his heel, his grey eyes alight.

'I've an alternative suggestion, Colonel. I entreat your most serious consideration.' He was speaking more rapidly than usual. 'Drury's plan is done with. On that we are agreed. It was always impracticable, because it demanded conditions which are unlikely in the extreme on this coast, at this season. My suggestion requires only that this westerly shall moderate. And it is moderating, Colonel. Within four days there may be a chance of success, of achieving our objective – of destroying the Dutch fleet.'

The colonel stared incredulously. 'Impossible, sir! There can be no alternative. And another four days of this will incapacitate such few of my men as are still—'

'Hear me out, Colonel, I beg. We assume the chance of the gale moderating to a fresh breeze. The moon is in her last quarter and the sky continues overcast. I lead my ships of the line, by night, directly into the Texel. Your regiments will be ready in the boats, towing astern. With good fortune and a dark night, the ships will be well within cannon-shot before the alarm is given. They will engage the forts with their broadsides, and at the same time the boats will cast off and land the military on the north and south shores of the gut. Instead of the land assault of Drury's plan, there will be a double assault on the Texel and Helder forts – by ships and by landing-parties.'

Doyle was listening open-mouthed, the picture of astonishment. He had never suspected the Admiral of entertaining the idea of so rash an enterprise. Nor, for the matter of that, had Adam Duncan. It was true he had toyed with the idea a year ago and dismissed it as folly. But now he saw it as the one chance of success left to them. By resolutely stifling his objections and flinging himself heart and soul into Uncle Henry's mad plan, he had insensibly come to covet its triumph as a miser covets gold. Now that Doyle wanted to turn tail, he saw his work wasted, his dogged patience of the past fortnight brought to nothing – and the Dutch Fleet still safe and snug in its anchorage. To attain what had become his own chief desire – the destruction of that fleet – he was ready now to be as rash as any young frigate captain. With a vague surprise, he heard himself rushing on.

'There is no surf within the entrance and the landings should be effected without any difficulty. The attentions of the forts will be directed to the ships, which will greatly increase the opportunity of the assault parties in the first instance, while the military attack will soon disconcert the fire from the guns of the forts. If the leading ships should win through—'

'God damn it, sir!' Doyle sprang up and slammed his fist on the table, shivering an empty glass. 'The thing's mere desperation! I'll not consider it! I've told you my regiments are too cursed feeble to hold their cursed muskets!'

'Three days of moderate weather might remedy that.'

' "Might", sir – and the wind might moderate and the night might be overcast! Here's a deal of dependence on chance!'

'No more than in Captain Drury's plan.'

'And what of your ships? D'ye think they'll come off unscathed? The forts will pound 'em to splinters.'

'Some of them will suffer. The rest should come through.'

'And if they do? Suppose the assault fails – who's to take the regiments aboard again?'

'That was also a defect of Drury's plan. They must not fail.'

'Pah!' Doyle stamped away and back again. 'I've told you, sir, I won't consider it. I hold to that. Half the men are as weak as babes, the rations are nigh exhausted—'

'Very well, Colonel,' Duncan said quietly.

He had sat down again at the table with his hands folded in front of him. The big interlaced fingers were trembling slightly; he noticed it, and the tremor stopped.

'*Redoubt* has yet to join,' he said in his deep even voice. 'She will probably do so tomorrow. When she is here, I shall order her back to Yarmouth with *Ramillies, Eurus,* and *Montagu.* You will of course arrange for the disembarkation of the troops as you think fit, Colonel.'

Colonel Doyle had a fleeting sense of something lost, of a vanished opportunity. But of course he was in the right of it – no one could deny that.

'And you, sir?' he demanded, picking up his cloak.

'I shall remain here with the remainder of my squadron,' Duncan said without looking up. 'I have supplies for another three weeks, and something may yet be achieved.'

And so Mr. Dundas's expedition departed for England, having failed utterly. So would Adam Duncan's daring plan have failed, for the moderating wind was a temporary respite and in forty-eight hours the westerly gale was howling again. The Admiral brought his ships back to Yarmouth on November 27th, the final failure being the destruction of his last hope of achievement by three weeks of unrelenting storm. He was greatly chastened, seeing at last his futile stubbornness in opposition to the plans of Providence. He had rebelled against the predestined course and deserved punishment. As *Venerable*'s anchor cable roared out through the hawse-hole a boat pulled ashore from her. It carried a package addressed to the First Lord of the Admiralty and containing Admiral Duncan's resignation from command.

Earl Spencer's reply by return of post contained a sufficiently effective balm.

'*And so far,*' wrote Spencer, '*from having lost any confidence in you in consequence from what has passed, my opinion of your judgment ought in fact to be increased, as it has turned out to be (what was most likely) much more correct than mine. I desire therefore that you will not think of such a measure as you talk of in your letter to me, which letter I shall show to no one but Mr. Dundas, to whom I this morning showed it, and who entirely agrees with me in thinking that the command entrusted to you cannot possibly be placed in better hands.*'

## FIVE

### I

*'Oct. 10, 1797. 11 a.m. Wind N.E., squally. Texel about 27 miles E.S.E.'*

The Admiral looked meditatively at the brief entry he had just made in his private log, while he waited for the ink to dry. The date caught his eye. That was another thing to be included in the First Lord's scheme of reforms for the Navy; the shipboard system of reckoning dates from one noon to the next was ridiculously confusing when reports came to be collated with the records kept on land. For everyone except seamen this was October 11th.

There was a thunderous knock on his cabin door. He had told Burnet a score of times to enter without knocking, yet the silly fellow insisted on banging as if he expected to find the Admiral engaged with a mistress.

'Come in, Mr. Burnet,' he called, repressing his impatience.

The Admiral's Secretary was a little man neatly habited in black, with steel-rimmed spectacles and the strut and bearing of a cock-sparrow.

'In the matter, sir, of that memorandum,' he announced as soon as he was inside the door. 'It was your wish that I should draft it as soon as possible. Anticipating much work for my humble self later today, to wit divers reports and lists *in re* the – um – victory which we pray will—'

'I fancy you'll not be plagued with that today, Mr. Burnet,' Duncan interrupted with a smile. 'If Mynheer De Winter is indeed at sea we're unlikely to come up with him before tomorrow morning. However, I beg you'll proceed with the draft letter to their Lordships. Submit, humbly pray and so forth – you know the phrases – and I think you have the facts.'

'I believe so, sir. A hundred and eighty mutineers at present confined in the hulks at Chatham. We ask a pardon. A free pardon, sir?'

'A free pardon.' Duncan nodded emphatically. 'These

poor fellows, Burnet, were misguided children, not pirates. It is easy to be misguided when you cannot read or write, when you've starved for most of your life, when you are liable to be flogged to death at another man's whim. Don't put that in your draft, though,' he added with a twinkle of his grey eyes.

'No, sir,' Burnet said gravely.

'And, Burnet,' the Admiral went on as the Secretary turned to leave the cabin, 'leave the draft incomplete. It may be that I shall have something to add.'

When the door had closed behind Burnet he remained sitting motionless at his desk, reflecting on the possibility of making that addition. If he were to beat the Dutch, he would have the more chance of persuading Admiralty to free the 180 men from the hulks; Spencer at any rate would be glad enough to rid himself of this last reminder of the Navy's darkest hour. Duncan had paid an unofficial visit to the hulks and knew all the horror of them – the filth, the vermin, the corruption and unnatural vice. He drew in his breath sharply as he thought of seamen, some of them from his own command, enduring that living hell; and for a moment the longed-for battle with the Dutch Fleet seemed chiefly important as a means of freeing them. Perhaps (he thought) his persistence on the men's behalf before and during the mutiny would in the long run do more for England than a victory at sea. He was quite certain that the Authority he thought of as God and spoke of as Providence would count it the greater work of the two.

But the destruction of De Winter's ships was of immediate and vital importance to the safety of his country – to her continued existence, indeed; and it had yet to be accomplished. He closed his private logbook and used it to hold open the chart on which it was lying. If De Winter had not by now got back into the Texel anchorage, where in all this fifteen hundred square miles of sea and shoal and treacherous bank could he be found?

The North Sea to northward of the Yarmouth-Texel line could be ruled out with fair certainty. If an invasion was indeed contemplated no seaman would try to get transports across in October by any of the longer crossings. True, the report from Halkett of the *Circe*, brought to Yarmouth by the *Speculator* lugger, had spoken of the Dutch ships sailing 'closehauled to the northward and westward' on the 8th, but De Winter might well steer a little north of west to clear his own difficult coast before heading south or south-west or west. So he was to be looked for down towards the Hook, or even north of that considering the transports would hamper him. There was a fair chance of catching him. British ships with their deeper keels could outsail the shallow-draught Dutchmen on a wind, and supposing the two fleets met *here,* or by the Middle Bank—

With his big forefinger on the chart, the Admiral checked himself. It was useless, even a shade impious, to speculate thus when Providence had already decreed the position of the Dutch Fleet. A devout Presbyterian would be better employed in praying for a speedy meeting and a victorious outcome of it. The Admiral had in fact begun to raise his eyes heavenward when his glance lighted upon the bookshelf on the bulkhead above the desk, and the worn calf binding of James Clerk's *Essay on Naval Tactics.* His thoughts were diverted. Would he have the courage – or the foolhardiness – to put into practice that idea of Clerk's? He had his two Divisions, with Vice-Admiral Onslow in *Monarch* to lead the van; and Onslow knew the possibility he had in mind. The Admiral himself was on the whole averse to experiment, especially in a battle of such moment as the one he hoped to bring about. The thing that dwelt in his mind was that by the adroit use of Clerk's theory he might turn the scales between an indecisive battle and a crushing victory. It would, of course, be extremely dangerous tactics if he found the Dutch close in with an onshore wind—

Again he halted himself. The Lord of Hosts was more likely to help him than was James Clerk of Eldin. But his ascending eye was caught by the miniature of his wife that hung above the bookshelf, and he could not help wondering whether he was in Henrietta's thoughts at this moment. If it was not raining in Yarmouth she would be taking a walk with young Henry. He was glad she had their youngest son for a companion; Henry was her favourite, he knew, though he was the least clever of the boys. Alexander was under the wing of Robert Dundas, now Lord Advocate, and showing great promise. Twelve-year-old Robert Duncan was staying with the Haldanes and seemed to be heading for the Army. Henry (his father smiled at his own conclusion) would probably enter the Navy.

Some sudden and indefinable change in *Venerable* whipped his thoughts away from domestic matters. It was a moment or two before he realized that the pumps, whose ceaseless dull thud and clank had made the background of his morning's work in the cabin, had stopped working. Duncan's thick brows drew down. He had made it plain to Fairfax that those pumps must be kept at work if the flagship was to remain manageable in a fight. With some hundreds of tons of water in her bilges she would be— The pumps had started again; new batch of men, probably ill-doers undergoing punishment, had taken over. With a slight shock he saw by the deck-head chronometer that it was half-a-minute past noon.

Perceiving that he was in no very prayerful mood, he went on deck. The weather was still overcast and squally, but the rain had stopped. The First Lieutenant had the quarterdeck and with him were the Master, Paterson, and the Pilot. Duncan approved of Paterson, who was a Fifeshire man and solid; but he mentally stigmatized Porteous, the Pilot, as a feckless body. Porteous came to him now, a gangling rawboned fellow with a shifty and apprehensive eye. He had to report that they were across the Broad Fourteens and passing the north tip of the Keg, and that he feared they were approaching the Texel on a falling tide. Duncan got rid of him as quickly as he could. It was like Porteous, he reflected as he turned to meet Cleland, to know the names and soundings of every North Sea bank and shudder each time he passed them.

'Ten of the line in company, sir,' Cleland said, showing white teeth in a smile. 'Full complement.'

'Thank you, Mr. Cleland.'

The First Lieutenant touched his cocked hat and strode easily away to the lee rail. Cleland would go far; he was a competent officer and knew precisely how much to say and leave unsaid. The words *'full complement'* were unnecessary, but they conveyed to a nicety Lieutenant Cleland's own satisfaction, his pleasure in the satisfaction Admiral Duncan must feel, and his feeling that even with eleven ships of the line Admiral Duncan was a match for Admiral De Winter. From beside the weather rail Duncan could see all the ships of his squadron and admire their superb grace and dignity as they sped under a press of canvas across the grey sea, each at the same angle of list, like a group of gigantic ballerinas. Eleven ships. Thirteen with *Russell* and *Adamant* when they reached the Texel. The necessary pause while he 'looked in' there should enable *Powerful, Agincourt,* and *Veteran* to come up with him. Sixteen ships of the line. Old and cranky as most of them were, they would give a good account of themselves in a ship-to-ship battle with the Dutch. But he needed more than a good account this time; he needed a conclusive, an absolute victory. This was where James Clerk's method might prove the turning-point – but the Admiral did not want to think about that just yet.

The cessation of the rain had brought *Venerable*'s upper deck into a state of great activity. On the lee side Major Trollope was holding an inspection of his Marines, and the line of scarlet coats with their pipeclayed belts and cross-straps brought a welcome touch of colour to the grey monochrome of sea and sky. Cresey, the boatswain, had several parties of seamen reeving and adjusting the recoil-ropes of the weather side twelve-pounders. Cresey's magnificent black pigtail (he was inordinately proud of that) flapped comically up and down as he delivered himself of an angry reprimand. The seaman he was addressing was smallish and foxy-faced, and he seemed to be standing up to the big boatswain – with some humorous rejoinder, judging from the grins on his shipmates' faces. That was Frowde. Duncan watched with interest. Cresey swung his fist, but it was a feint blow and not intended to land; clearly Frowde's jest had amused him. He moved on to the next party, leaving Frowde hard at work with his chuckling fellows.

The Admiral nodded contentedly to himself. The little scene had been reassuring. He wondered whether Frowde jested about the time Admiral Duncan had drawn his sword upon him; and whether Frowde realized how near he had come to being run through.

He swung round to gaze at the ships of his squadron again, but his thoughts had gone back to a day six months ago. He liked to think that *Venerable*'s men would never have attempted mutiny had they known his efforts on their behalf. Yet if that was so it ran counter to his lifelong rule – never to seek publicity for his doings. He had sought amendment for their condition over and over again during the past two years – aye, and long before then. He had pestered the Admiralty, warned the First Lord a score of times. 'Ships are men,' he had told Spencer, with a paradoxical turn of phrase that sounded odd in retrospect. And the ships that were with him now were composed of men who had been in a state of mutiny just nineteen weeks ago; except for *Venerable* and *Adamant*. He had that morning been reckoning his sixteen of the line, and his guns, and his James Clerk tactics – but what use were these if his men should fail him?

He remembered how cocksure he had been on that April morning, a week before the terrible day when he had had Frowde at his sword-point. The spring sunshine had been bright and warm on the pavements of Whitehall, but the shadow of the great mutiny was already spreading above the rooftops of the Admiralty. . . .

## II

In the anteroom the light filtered weakly through the grimy windows. By contrast the handsome chamber to which the Admiral was admitted was brilliantly lit. The sunbeams played freely through panes newly cleansed of London soot, emphasizing the gold braid in the dark portraits on the walls and flashing from the polished mahogany of desk and chairs. Earl Spencer, at the desk, rose to extend a hand to Duncan. The smile of welcome on his lean face was warm enough, but his clerks would have recognized the closing of the gap between his greying eyebrows as a sign of impatience.

'Good morning, my dear Admiral,' he said affably. 'You are becoming as great an *habitué* here as I am myself. Let me hasten to add that the pleasure of seeing you—'

'I am importunate, I know,' said Duncan; the stout chair groaned as he lowered himself into it. 'Importunate, sir, in a most urgent cause.'

'Of course, of course,' said Spencer quickly. 'Mrs. Duncan is well? I hear she is in Town.'

'She travelled with me from Yarmouth. My ships refitting there will complete in two days' time and I return tomorrow, to await your lordship's orders for sea.'

Spencer nodded approval. 'You may receive those before

very long. Our information is that troops are being moved to the Texel for embarkation.'

'Good news indeed, sir. The sooner we meet them the better. I would not have left Yarmouth but for these rumours from Spithead. Have they any substance, my lord?'

The First Lord allowed his frowning gaze to dwell on the big old man sitting opposite to him. It crossed his mind that the commander-in-chief of the North Sea Fleet carried his years very well, in spite of that mane of snow-white hair. (Henry Dundas jested that his nephew-by-marriage from Dundee saved a fortune in hair-powder every year.) It was probably the unfailingly erect bearing, together with that quite unconscious grace of his, that gave him his characteristic air of unassuming dignity – the height of contrast, come to think of it, with that vain little monkey Nelson. But Spencer's liking and admiration for Duncan were no obstacle to his finding old Adam a confounded nuisance; especially after this business at Spithead. No man likes to be in a position where another can justly cry 'I told you so'. Earl Spencer was no exception to this rule.

'The news from Spithead is rumour no longer,' he said abruptly. 'On Easter Sunday the Channel Fleet refused to put to sea. I went down within forty-eight hours to meet their damned delegates, as they call 'em. I offered them three shillings a month extra and they refused it.'

'Extra pay won't redress their wrongs,' Duncan muttered.

Spencer ignored him. 'I offered again, in different form. It was read on all ships by the senior officers – still aboard their own ships on sufferance, believe it or not – and the mutinous rogues deigned to tell me they'd consider it only when I'd obtained a Royal Pardon for their actions. I drove post-haste back to London and got their precious Pardon.'

'That was well done.'

'I beg leave to doubt that, sir. With the French and the Dutch at our gates we must have the Fleet at sea or perish, and submission seemed my only course.' The First Lord clenched his fists. 'I should have turned the fortress guns on 'em. The knaves received their Pardon and their three shillings and still refused to sail. Their delegates still command the Channel Fleet, with Bridport helpless and every officer *persona non grata*. And Our Lordships of the Admiralty—' he raised his arms and let them fall.

The Admiral fingered his big square chin.

'They asked other things besides the increase in pay, surely,' he said with a lift of his brows.

'A few matters of small moment,' Spencer said absently. He levelled a forefinger suddenly. 'Do you know what I smell in this business, sir? The hand of the Revolution! French agents – or more likely English traitors in French pay! Or why should the men not accept His Majesty's pardon and the Admiralty's grant of extra money?'

'Have you any evidence of French interference?' the Admiral asked.

'None. I admit it. But as an explanation of the causes of this most untoward—'

'For the causes, sir,' said Duncan, breaking in with unwonted sharpness, 'you need look no farther than an English ship of the line. What, pray, were the few matters of small moment you spoke of just now?'

The First Lord waved a hand irritably. 'Flour for bread, fresh vegetables, an abatement of flogging – things of that kind. And I fancy there was a demand for doctors for the sick men.'

'In short, sir, they asked their just dues,' Duncan nodded. 'If money was their prime demand, it would be merely natural. They do not grumble that their pay is nineteen shillings a month – precisely what it was in Oliver Cromwell's day. They grumble, indeed, when they aren't paid at all. My lads aboard *Monmouth* received their last money eighteen months ago. I have applied on their behalf, and without result. I am not, let me add, blaming your lordship for this neglect.'

'Thank you, sir,' Spencer interpolated drily.

'But your three shillings did nothing for their real needs, which are the needs of any human creature – clean food, care in sickness, a curb on the inhumanity of their masters.'

'By which high-sounding phrase,' the First Lord observed with a curl of the lip, 'you mean, I presume, the abolishment of flogging.'

'No, my lord. Nor do the seamen demand that. I mean the observance by all captains of the Admiralty regulation – a maximum punishment of two dozen lashes.'

'You accuse sea officers of ignoring the regulation?'

'Pray let us be frank, my lord. You know as well as I do that captains – not all, but many – will order two-score, fifty, a hundred lashes without awaiting instruction from a Court Martial.'

Spencer lowered his eyes to the desk. 'This matter is under present consideration,' he said testily. 'We have to go delicately. The principle of a captain's absolute authority on board his own ship must not be undermined.'

Duncan shifted his massive bulk impatiently and leaned forward. His deliberate utterance was in marked contrast with the other man's brusque manner.

'I agree – but it's undermined already. A seaman's absolute obedience to orders is assured if he knows that his officers, the captain included, are under the same discipline as himself. Every seaman knows but too well that this is not so. He can be flogged to death, starved to death, allowed to die of disease without attention, at the whim of his commanding officer. He has no hope of redress, no appeal beyond that same commanding officer. The most beggarly Englishman ashore has more assurance of—'

'But good God, sir!' Spencer exploded. 'You above all should know what manner of men we have to deal with! Pressed men, the sweepings of gaols and brothels. Brute beasts with no understanding of aught but the lash.'

Duncan's grey eyes flashed. 'But men, my lord. Seamen, if the Navy deals justly with them, after a month's service.'

'You speak of Englishmen,' the First Lord swept on unheeding. 'Look at your ships' companies, man – Portuguese, Swedes, black men, even French and Dutch and Spanishers. Sixty per cent English, if that. And d'ye tell me true Englishmen would stab their country in the back as these damned fellers at Spithead have done?' He slammed his clenched fist on the desk. 'By heaven, they're using England's need as a weapon against her! And this when I'm moving heaven and earth and the Treasury to get 'em better ships!'

'Better ships,' repeated the Admiral; his deep voice took on a resonant note. 'Ships are men, my lord. A shell of timber, even if it's heart of oak, is made into a ship – a fighting ship – by those who man her. Look first to the men. Whether they know it or not, the damned fellers at Spithead are giving you the course you should steer.'

'So! You'd have the Admiralty take orders from mutinous seaman! This is—'

'I'd have you move heaven and earth – and the Treasury

– to set right the men's just grievances. If you don't, and that directly, this mutiny will spread beyond Spithead.'

Two bright red patches had appeared on the First Lord's thin cheeks. He gripped the edge of the desk with both hands and half-rose on his feet, his eyes narrowing.

'By heaven, Admiral Duncan!' he said between his teeth. 'I think you side with the mutineers, do you not? Perhaps you hold your ships at Yarmouth ready to support this Spithead rising?'

Duncan's big face darkened. He bit his lip to hold back the angry retort that was on the tip of his tongue.

'I believe you know me better than that, my lord,' he said quietly. 'I am a King's officer. Mutiny is a crime against His Majesty. I would plunge my sword into the heart of a ringleader who outfaced me aboard one of my ships. I tell you but the plain fact that the cause of the mutiny is Admiralty neglect.'

Spencer got up abruptly and strode across to the window, where he stood with his back to the room and his bony hands twisted tightly together. The Admiral went on speaking, in the same even tone.

'If they are using this country's need as a weapon, as you suggest, it's a defensive weapon against abuse – and they use it because they have no other. You and I realize, as the men do not, the extent of England's danger. We know that if the mutiny spreads, if the invader strikes from the Texel while the Navy is out of action, we are at the mercy of the French. For that reason the mutiny must be put down instantly, by any means at our command. The most effective means, believe me, would be the immediate redress of all grievances. But if force has to be used you may count on me, my lord, as on yourself.'

The First Lord spun round and came striding back to his desk. The red blotches had gone from his face, leaving it paler than usual.

'I beg you'll accept my apology, Admiral Duncan,' he said formally. 'My words were spoken in heat and I hope you'll forget them.'

'They are forgotten already, my lord.'

'Thank you. Then I needn't add that I know of no servant of His Majesty less likely to abet rebellion.' A transient smile crinkled Spencer's lips. 'I never thought to hear you make so long a speech, Adam. And I grant the general truth of what you say. I am already moving to better the seaman's lot, but you know as well as I do that these reforms take time.'

Duncan nodded gloomily. 'Precisely. But there's no time left. The sands have run out.'

'I pray that you are wrong. But I know, Adam, that I can rely on you. Can you, in turn, rely on your ships – in the unlikely event of this infection of mutiny spreading?'

The Admiral hesitated for the fraction of a second. It was on the tip of his tongue to remind the First Lord that the constituents of the North Sea Fleet were continually being changed, so that he had little chance of getting to know his officers or the ships' companies; that the ships themselves were manned by the refuse of London, with the merest nucleus of trained and loyal seamen. But Spencer knew these things already.

'I will answer for my Fleet, my lord,' he said, getting up and taking his cocked hat from the desk. 'You may depend on me to keep order.'

'I shall do so, sir.' Spencer held out his hand. 'You'll be kept informed of matters at Spithead. My duty to Mrs. Duncan, if you please. And be easy, Adam. I'm assured that a firm hand will rout the malcontents and that will be the end of the matter.'

But the Admiral was not easy. As he stalked out to his waiting carriage, with the Whitehall idlers crowding to admire his huge and handsome figure, the dark cloud on his brow was in ominous contrast to the April sunshine.

## III

On the afternoon of April 30th, seven days after his visit to Earl Spencer, Admiral Duncan sat at his desk in his cabin on board *Venerable*. The summer of 1797 seemed to have come before its time, for the hot sunlight on deck made the cabin warm in spite of the open stern windows, and the anchorage off Yarmouth was so calm that no motion or sound of any kind disturbed the Admiral's re-reading of Earl Spencer's letter. He was frowning as he read. It was only too clear that Spencer thought a few concessions and the vague promise of more had solved the problem of Spithead; but the ships there were in fact still refusing discipline, and the First Lord's casual mention of disturbances in the squadron stationed at Plymouth was not reassuring. He laid the letter on the desk with a sigh and threw himself back impatiently in his chair – to start bolt upright a second later, listening.

There had been a distant shout in a man's high tenor voice. It was followed instantly by a far louder sound – the roar of hundreds of voices upraised in three lusty cheers. Three unauthorized cheers, he recalled, had begun the mutiny aboard the Spithead flagship, *Queen Charlotte*.

The Admiral moved with an agility surprising in a man of his years. He was out of the cabin before the marine sentry could come to attention, and narrowly avoided cannoning into Cleland, who came rushing towards him along the alleyway.

'It's the men, sir,' Cleland panted. 'All on deck without orders. It looks like—'

'Major!' Duncan had espied Major Trollope's bulky figure beyond the First Lieutenant. 'Muster your men amidships instantly. Mr. Cleland, my sword from the cabin if you please.'

Trollope hurried away at the double-march. Cleland took less than ten seconds to fetch the Admiral's sword, but before Duncan had buckled it on the startling *rafale* of the marines' drum was reverberating through the ship. On the heels of that came the irregular thunder of the redcoats' boots on the ladder leading from their quarters. The last scarlet coats with their white crossbelts were scurrying into double rank abaft the mainmast as the Admiral, with Cleland at his shoulder, emerged into the bright sunlight on deck.

The scene before him was striking in its mass and colour. Looking forward below the spread of the bare yards, beyond the massive round of the mainmast and the hedge of vivid scarlet uniforms beside it, he saw a great throng of men: men hatless or covered, in loose trousers and blouses of every hue; men big and small, brownfaced or pallid or Negro-black; men swarming like bees in the foremast shrouds and packed from bulwark to bulwark across foredeck and fo'c'sle head. Duncan stalked for'ard past the line of squat twelve-pounders, past the equally rigid marines – receiving Major Trollope's salute on the way – until he reached the three officers who fronted the crowd of men.

They were two lieutenants, Renton and Little, and Paterson the Master. Mr. Darby, the Admiral's chaplain, stood (or rather, hopped nervously) just behind them. Captain Fairfax was ashore. There were some five hundred and fifty men congregated on deck and in the shrouds, and the noise of muttered or shouted interruptions quite drowned whatever harangue Renton was making.

The Admiral strode straight past his officers, aware that the noise subsided as soon as he appeared. When he was ten paces away from the foremost men in the throng (their front rank formed a fairly straight line, as if they sought to maintain a kind of order) he halted and stood with his legs apart, his hands behind him, and his great head thrown back.

'Well?' The great voice hurled the single word at them, and in the brief pause that followed there was utter silence. 'I wait to hear your reason for this improper conduct.'

There was a shifting, a rustling and whispering as of forest leaves stirred by a wind, but no one answered him.

'I order you to disperse to your quarters.'

Again there was muttering and restless movement, but no response. Duncan's grey eyes flashed and his lip curled.

'You won't obey me, and you're afraid to speak to me – is that it? Have you no men among you who'll speak?'

As though pushed forward by the pressure of the rest, five seamen stood out in the front. One of them was a slight fellow with red hair and a foxy face that Duncan recognized; Frowde was his name, and a month ago he had received six lashes at Fairfax's order for assaulting two of the ship's boys.

'We don't obey orders no longer,' Frowde said truculently in a loud, high voice that was certainly the voice that had called for the cheers.

'You are the leader of this – this nonsense, Frowde?'

The man looked startled. 'Me and these others here,' he said. 'We demand our rights, and if we don't get 'em—'

'You know this is mutiny, Frowde?' Duncan said, loudly enough for all to hear.

Frowde raised his own voice. ''Tain't mutiny! We demand our rights, I said. There's no orders'll be obeyed till we get 'em.'

'The punishment for mutineers is death.' As he spoke, the Admiral's left hand gripped his scabbard and pulled it across his thigh. 'For me, if I don't put down a mutiny instantly, the punishment is the same – death. That's His Majesty's law for his Navy, and—'

'Damn your talk!' Frowde shrilled, gesticulating fiercely. 'We mean to haul down yer flag, old man, and if you wants to save yer neck—'

Duncan whipped out his sword and took two long strides forward. The point gleamed in the sun, two inches from Frowde's chest. Next moment the chaplain had hurled himself at the Admiral and was clinging to his sword-arm, gibbering hysterically, and the front ranks of the seamen displayed a gap where the terrified Frowde had burst through to hide himself in the throng.

Afterwards, inevitably, Duncan came to look upon Mr. Darby as the predestined agent of Providence. As the voice of the angel prevented Abraham's sacrifice of Isaac, so had the chaplain's grasp prevented the slaughter of one of those whom he regarded as his children; for he would have held by the word he had given to Spencer, alien though the action would have been to his nature. Indeed, the very result of Darby's intervention demonstrated the Almighty wisdom. Frowde's tragi-comic exit touched some humorous chord in his shipmates, and though a few flung half-hearted threats at the Admiral there were many more who chuckled. Duncan shook the chaplain from his arm as if he were a too-affectionate dog and sheathed his sword.

'Major Trollope!' he roared; Trollope clanked and clattered to his side. 'Be ready to obey my order on the instant. – Now, my lads! Your five leaders – and that includes Mr. Frowde, if he can be found – will be taken to the poop where I can talk with them quietly. The rest of you will go to your quarters when I give the word. – Disperse!'

No man spoke. Every man moved. The shrouds emptied, the companionways echoed to the thud of bare feet as several hundred seamen went quietly below decks. The men of the anchor watch remained on deck, and presently five sheepish-looking men stood before the Admiral, who had not moved his position an inch. The largest of the five held Frowde's arm in a tight grip.

'Thank you, Major. You may dismiss your men.' Duncan turned on his heel and spoke to the First Lieutenant. 'Have them to the poop, Mr. Cleland, if you please.'

'Get aft, you lot!' snapped Cleland in no very gentle voice.

As he walked slowly aft himself Duncan became aware of the great ships lying at anchor near the flagship, with low green land lying beyond them across the shimmer of the Roads. If this could happen on board his own *Venerable*, what might not happen in *Nassau* and *Adamant* and the rest? And he had been so cocksure when he was talking to Spencer! In the whole of his life Adam Duncan had never felt himself so humbled. It was with a heavy heart, if with an impassive countenance, that he went through with the plan he had determined upon.

Without a glance at the five ringleaders, now standing beside Cleland at the break of the poop, he mounted the ladder to the quarterdeck and turned.

'Pipe all hands aft, Mr. Cleland, if you please.'

The First Lieutenant could not repress his quick glance of astonishment, but he gave the order immediately and was echoed by Cresey's roar. The pipes of the bosun's mates twittered. Major Trollope came trotting to the Admiral and was bidden to hold his men ready below decks, out of sight; the marines had played their part – they had mustered on deck in record time, Duncan thought – and he had no wish to over-emphasize the threat of loyal redcoats with muskets. Now the ship was vibrating again to the rush of feet as the hands poured up on deck. There had been no hesitation in obeying that order and indeed he had expected none. Directed by Cleland, boatswain and quartermasters got larboard and starboard watches massed on the deck between mainmast and poop. Duncan ran his eye over the hundreds of upturned faces and saw uncertainty, apprehension, curiosity; they must be wondering at this summons a few minutes after they had been sent below.

Cleland mounted the ladder and with an emphatic salute reported all hands assembled. The Admiral sent him to stand by the after rail with the rest of his officers, and then descended with a firm and stately tread to the deck where the five ringleaders were standing. There was some murmuring from the crowd of seamen as he began to question the five, but the murmurs were instantly silenced by those standing near them and the deep resonant voice rang in a breathless silence.

Frowde, his foxy face very pale, made no answer and

kept his eyes on the deck. It was a big seaman with tousled fair hair (Duncan did not know his name, nor did he ask it) who replied to the Admiral's questions. He denied that *Venerable*'s crew were mutineers. Their friends at Spithead had given three cheers and they saw no harm in doing the same. It was because they wanted to know when their increased pay and provisions was to commence. That was all, yer Honour.

Duncan spoke very briefly and simply. The new rates of pay, he told them, had already been ordered by the Admiralty and would come into force at once. They would get extra money the next time they were paid. As for provisions, the suppliers on shore had had their instructions – and he trusted the purser would not increase his takings accordingly. There was a subdued ripple of laughter at this; pursers were believed, with some justification, to sell a proportion of the ship's provisions for their own profit. A sudden sternness of tone in the Admiral's voice swiftly quelled the laughter. When a ship's company acted without orders, or refused to obey an order, that was mutiny, according to the regulations of His Majesty King George the Third. He, Admiral Duncan, had power to administer the extreme penalty for the crime of mutiny. That penalty was death. (Duncan paused a moment here; the silence was absolute.) It was also in his power to pardon offenders, if he thought fit. In the present case he believed they had acted in error, meaning no harm and without knowledge of what they were doing, and on condition of nothing of this kind happening again he would freely pardon the ship's company and the five seamen who appeared to be their leaders.

The sign of pent breath escaping from his audience was audible as he concluded, but Duncan allowed no opportunity for more than that.

'Major Trollope!'

'Sir!' The Major marched forward and clicked his heels.

'I wish to commend you and your men publicly for the promptitude and loyalty displayed by the marines in this matter. I shall make it my business to inform their Lordships at the Admiralty of it. – Mr. Cleland, dismiss the men if you please.'

So was the mutiny of the *Venerable* put down. But not Adam Duncan's grief and concern. Until late that evening the door of the Admiral's cabin remained locked; and Mr. Darby the chaplain averred with a fearful joy that the Admiral was seeking solace in prayer.

Solace in a different form came later that week. A painfully written screed of six sheets found its way to Duncan's desk. It began: *'Most worthy and honoured Sir, – Not having the gift of speech of accosting you in a proper manner we the ship's company of H.M. ship "Venerable" having taken into consideration the weighty affair which was so indiscreetly committed on the 30th ult. and for which we are sincearly ashamed of we theirfore think it our duty to return you our most sincear and hearty thanks for forgiving us the rash step which we took on that fatel day*'; continued with apologies for the offence given to '*the wortheyest of commanders who as proved a father to us*'; and concluded with prayers to be protected from any more '*diabolical practices*' of the kind and vows that if the Admiral led them against the enemy '*their his not one man on board of the "Venerable" but what would lose the last drop of blood in his body before they should obtain any victory over us.*' This, and his success in wresting the men's dues from rascally merchants and reluctant paymasters, brought Duncan a deal of comfort. He could count on *Venerable* at least, even if the mutiny were to spread.

And spread it did, to a quite unanticipated extent. At Spithead and Plymouth the affair was quietly over; but before Bridport and the Channel Fleet sailed for the blockade of Brest with the Union flag once more flying from every masthead, the ships at the Nore had all mutinied under their leader the demagogue Richard Parker. The Nore ships sent their 'delegates' in a cutter to Yarmouth, and their news – that they had put their officers ashore and hoisted the red flag in every ship at the great anchorage off Sheerness – was enough to start a ferment in the vessels of the North Sea Fleet. A fortnight after the affair on board *Venerable* the ominous cheering was heard from the 50-gun *Adamant*. Duncan had himself rowed across immediately and found Captain Hotham and his lieutenants, with their swords drawn, fronting the whole crew massed on the foredeck. The Admiral ordered them to put up their swords, and set himself between them and the seamen.

'My lads,' said he, 'in all my service I've maintained my authority. I warn you I shan't part with it easily. Now – is there any man here who dares to dispute that authority?'

There was a moment's pause, and then a stocky seaman stepped forward, urged from behind by his shipmates but assuming a bold air.

'I do, old cock,' he said, glancing round for approval.

The glance was his undoing. Duncan took him by the collar of his tight jersey and lifted him off his feet, to hold him up at arm's length as he had done with a certain 'friend of the people' twenty-one years ago in Maundy Place. Exerting all his magnificent strength, he bore his captive to the rail, swung him over it, and dangled him above the green water.

'Here's your leader, men!' he roared at them. 'Here's the man who'd deprive me of the command of my Fleet! Will you follow him – if I let him go?'

The confused uproar that greeted this gesture approved him. A voice called for 'a cheer for Old Adam', and the cheer was given with a will. Duncan swung the seaman back again, set him on his feet, and sent him towards his fellows with a gentle push before turning to Hotham.

'You may pipe down, Captain,' he said.

And that was the end of trouble in *Adamant*. But the ferment seethed on in *Lion* and *Nassau* and half a dozen others of the North Sea Fleet, encouraged by the success of the Nore mutineers. By May 22nd the Secretary of the Admiralty was writing, *The ships at the Nore are in the most complete state of mutiny*', and inquiring whether Admiral Duncan could depend on his ships if they were ordered to sail round and chastise the mutineers. Duncan replied without enthusiasm; to set British ships fighting each other was, to his mind, no solution of the trouble. He prayed every day that the orders fore-shadowed by Earl Spencer a month ago would arrive swiftly; in action alone did he see a clear chance of holding his Fleet together. And his prayers were answered.

*'(Secret) Downing Street: Sunday May 21, 1797*

*'Information relative to the state of the Dutch Navy in the Texel. Received May 20, 1797.*

*'There are now lying in the Texel ready for sea – 18 ships of the line; 22 frigates, sloops, and brigs, from 44 to 10 guns; 42 large transports fitting out for the reception of troops.*

*'There is little doubt of a descent upon this country being in contemplation.'*

The Foreign Office intelligence, a copy of which reached Admiral Duncan on May 22nd, was followed four days later by Admiralty orders to sail at once for the Texel. In the morning of May 27th *Venerable* weighed anchor and hoisted all plain sail to catch the light and variable westerly wind. From her quarterdeck the Admiral watched anxiously while ship after ship of the North Sea Fleet, obedient to his signal, got under way. *Adamant, Repulse, Lion; Standard, Agamemnon, Glatton, Isis, Monmouth, Ardent.* Only *Belliqueux* was not moving – and now she, too, was making sail. Duncan heaved a vast sigh of relief. The North Sea Fleet was at sea. With it, if the enemy invasion force sailed, he could save England.

# SIX

## I

'La-a-and ho! Fine on th' stabb'd bow!'

The hail from the flagship's masthead brought the Admiral out of his after-lunch reverie with a start. For three-quarters of an hour he had been marching up and down beside the quarterdeck rail, with his mind so occupied with the events of six months ago that he had to reassure himself, by a quick glance at the great ships following *Venerable* on either quarter, that all was well. For all had not been well when he had sailed from Yarmouth Roads at the end of May. Duncan found himself wondering whether Providence was about to compensate him for the humiliations and anxieties of that last cruise to the Texel. But did Providence compensate, in this world? *Their reward shall be in heaven,* he remembered. Well, it would be a black outlook for England if Adam Duncan were not fully rewarded within the next twenty-four hours – and in this world, not the next. The thought savoured of irreverence. He flung it hastily from him as Captain Fairfax came across the quarterdeck.

'A good landfall, sir,' Fairfax said, his square face imperturbable as ever under the squarely adjusted cocked hat. 'Mr. Cleland went aloft himself. He reports it's certainly the Texel, about four leagues—'

'Sa-a-il!' Again came the aerial voice. 'Frigate, right ahead.' A pause, then – 'It's *Circe*, sir – closin' fast!'

There was a buzz of eager comment from the officers on the quarterdeck. *Circe* had been left with *Russell* and *Adamant* to watch the Texel. It was certain she would know the whereabouts of the two ships of the line, who had not yet been sighted, and it was just possible that she could tell the Admiral where to find the Dutch Fleet. Duncan leaned out across the weather rail to catch a first sight of her.

The rain had held off since noon, but the grey clouds still sped threateningly above a rolling grey sea. To Duncan's eye, familiar with these waters, the sign of shoal water was obvious – a yellowish grey overside instead of the greener grey of the sea west of Brown Bank. There was a mere ten or twelve fathoms under *Venerable*'s keel here. It was not long before he saw *Circe*'s fore topsail rising like a wraith on the eastern rim of the grey waste. With asonishing rapidity her courses hove in sight, and then she was hull-up. Soon she was closing the flagship, a lovely sight with her low clean lines and spread of sail. Duncan glanced up at the yardarm. Maxwell had hoisted *Circe*'s pendant with Number 47 below it – 'come within hail'. A minute later the signal to heave-to, preceded by the General pendant, set all eleven ships of the line busily furling main courses. *Venerable,* her towering wings trimmed by the ant-like creatures swarming along the yards, shuddered and slowed and rocked uneasily as she lost way.

*Circe* came surging past on the opposite course, foamed round in a full turn, and was laid neatly hove-to a cable's length away on the flagship's weather beam. Her captain's long lean figure was clinging to the lower main shrouds.

'Flagship ahoy!' Halkett's voice, aided by his speaking trumpet, came quite loudly downwind. 'No sign of the Dutch. *Russell* and *Adamant* cruising south'ard, looking for them.'

Duncan's eyes gleamed. They were still out, then. But could Halkett be perfectly sure of that? No one knew better than the Admiral how difficult it was to keep a continuous close watch on the Texel entrance. He swung round to call Fairfax, and then checked himself; he could make his voice carry as far as any man on board. Taking a high grip on the cordage of the mizzen shrouds, he swung himself up until he was standing on the rail.

'Captain Halkett!' He saw Halkett lift his hat. 'Send a boat. I'm coming on board you.'

Halkett waved his hat and vanished. Duncan could imagine the instant bustle in *Circe* – the boat's crew ordered away and hounded to their utmost speed, the hasty preparations for his reception. He gave Fairfax brief instructions – the Fleet was to maintain its station hove-to until he should return with *Circe* – and went below to get his boat-cloak.

When he came on deck again the frigate was no longer on the weather beam. Having sent his boat away, Halkett had brought his vessel round to the lee side so as to give the boat a speedier and easier passage back. *Circe* had been handled with the utmost efficiency and was already on the flagship's starboard beam; Halkett was a first-rate officer and a thoughtful one. Duncan clambered stiffly down into the tossing boat and was pulled across to the frigate, where the boatswain and his two mates were ready at the rail to pipe him aboard, with Halkett doffing his hat just beyond them. It was heartening to see the smile of genuine pleasure on Halkett's thin face. The moment formalities were over Duncan put his questions and received the succinct answers he expected.

The Dutch Fleet had sailed three days ago, taking advantage of the easterly wind, which had blown *Russell* and *Adamant* off station. *Circe* had made out sixteen sail of the line, five frigates, and five brigs – but no transports. Halkett had at once dispatched the *Speculator* lugger to Yarmouth with the news. Meanwhile, with *Russell* and *Adamant* in company again, the little squadron had dogged the slow progress of the Dutch ships on a westerly course, hampered by squalls and fitful winds, until in the calm and fog of the 10th they had lost touch. De Winter's ships had then been about seven leagues off the land about Wykop Zee and making very slowly to the south-west. Captain Trollope of the *Russell* had ordered the frigate back to the Texel in case the Dutch turned back under cover of the thick weather.

'The transports weren't with 'em, sir,' Halkett explained, 'so we couldn't tell what they were up to. Unless,' he added, 'they're waiting for you, sir – looking for a fight.'

The gleam in the Admiral's grey eyes answered the eager glint in the frigate captain's blue ones. That could well be so. If the Batavian Republic had resolved to get rid of the English blockade once for all, De Winter would have a better chance of victory without the transports.

'They are not returned into the Texel – you're sure of that?' he asked.

Halkett hesitated. 'There's no special activity in the entrance, sir. But my lookout spied your topsails before I'd had a clear view of the Mars Deep.'

'We must make perfectly certain, Captain. Make sail, if you please.'

'Aye aye, sir.'

It was delightful to feel the bound and heel of a frigate

under him in place of the stolid progress of a ship of the line. Duncan declined Halkett's suggestion that he should go below and remained on the narrow quarterdeck while *Circe* raced towards the Dutch coast. With a fresh breeze for'ard of the beam she was far faster than *Venerable*. In no time at all, it seemed, the low drab line of the coast was lifting on the horizon, and with the assurance of familiarity (*Circe* had cruised continuously off the Texel for twenty-three weeks) Halkett set his course to avoid the dangerous shoals that guarded the entrance. Now the pallor of the dunes could be seen edging the grey sea, with a darker rim above them marking the more solid land behind. The narrow break in this parti-coloured ribbon on the horizon was the Texel entrance, and at sight of it the Admiral's pulse quickened with an excitement that would better have suited someone fifty years his junior. For on that gut of waterway, little more than 2,500 yards across, the eyes of England had rested in fear for more than two years; and those of Adam Duncan in hope too often deferred.

*Circe* was lying as near the wind as she could to approach on a course north-east by east. A mile or less to larboard the sea was choppy and disordered, with a brownish look about the wavetops. That was the North Hack Sand that masked the entrance from the west. The bar of land on the left, now rapidly revealing its sparse details, was the Texel island itself; that on the right was the mainland of North Holland. Once through the gulf between them, you were free of a vast expanse of shallow inland seas, free to cross the Wieringer Meer and round Enkhuysens Point into the Zuyder Zee, with Amsterdam at your mercy – but only if you could get past the two forts that commanded the narrow entrance, and then you would have to have a vessel of small draught, a light and favourable wind, and a local pilot with unimpeachable knowledge of the channels. The forts alone (Duncan reflected for the hundredth time) were sufficient prohibition. At that short range the Texel and Helder forts between them had any ship at their mercy. He wondered at his recklessness of last year, when he had seriously proposed to sail into the entrance while Colonel Doyle's men stormed the forts.

'You can see the Texel fort now, sir,' Halkett said, crossing to stand beside him. 'And there's the Helder just coming into sight. We'll be in range in five minutes.'

'Hold your course for two minutes, then,' Duncan said. 'Heave-to out of range. And Captain Halkett – if I may borrow your glass? Mine is aboard *Venerable*.'

Halkett raised his thin brows. 'Of course, sir. But – you're not going aloft? I was thinking of taking a look from the foremast head—'

'I would prefer to take that look myself, Captain. I am still – um – reasonably spry.'

'Aye aye, sir. – Hullo, they've seen us.'

A puff of smoke had broken from the tiny grey shape that was barely discernible on the Texel side of the entrance. A few moments later they heard the dull boom of the gun, but there was no splash of falling shot to be seen. Halkett roared orders and the frigate came to the wind. With the borrowed glass in his coat pocket, the Admiral went for'ard and began to climb the foremast shrouds. At sixty-six, he felt, he could use the lubber's hole without inviting criticism from the seamen watching on the deck below. It was a young man's feat to climb the fore topgallant shrouds, but he did it, albeit slowly, and reached the exiguous wooden stance at the topgallant masthead. He was pleased to find that the effort of climbing a hundred and twenty feet had not unsteadied him in the least, and with one arm hooked round the spar he could focus the glass at once on his objective. The Texel fort stood out clearly now – it had not fired again – and beyond it he could see the widening strait of the anchorage, the Mars Deep, where alone was there water enough for a fleet to lie at anchor. A cutter was flitting across from the Helder side, and that was all. The Dutch Fleet was still at sea.

Duncan climbed slowly and steadily down again to the deck and gave Halkett his news. Admiral and captain grinned frankly at each other; there was no doubt now that their chance had come at last. *Circe* heeled as the helm brought her round and the wind sped her on her way back to the Fleet. It was two o'clock. By three, Duncan reflected, the chase would have begun. He had to find De Winter, but he had little doubt of that. And then – then there would be payment in full for all the frustrations of the past two years. Payment for his humiliation and anxiety during those five perilous days in June.

He was gazing astern, beyond *Circe*'s spreading wake to the fast-fading bar of the Texel. It was quite possible that his daring piece of trickery there in June had saved his country. Not that he thought of himself as a man of daring; it had been forced on him. The stunning blow that had fallen – and yet it should not have surprised him. It was odd, he reflected, how a man might know in his heart the probabilities of disaster and shut his mind to them, so that when the evil day came he could be as shocked by them as if they had never occurred to him. When he had come on deck that morning of 29th May (he would never forget that date) and had seen for himself that Fairfax's report was true. . . .

## II

'What's this, Captain?'

The Admiral strode to the larboard quarterdeck rail with unwonted haste. His Flag Captain, with a grim face, gestured silently towards the huge dim shape that moved slowly through the haze, a quarter of a mile away on *Venerable*'s larboard beam. Duncan gripped the rail and stood gazing, his huge body utterly motionless.

The sun was not yet up. Only the lightest of airs stirred the early morning haze that hung above the unrippled surface of the sea. Beyond the almost imperceptible undulations of the silken water the massive hulls and tall spars of the North Sea Fleet seemed suspended between sky and sea, as motionless as the Admiral himself. The south-easterly wind had fallen away outside the Yarmouth banks on the previous day and left them becalmed, so that Duncan – with that urgent order from the Admiralty driving him – had anxiety enough already. Now he saw one of his ships under sail without orders and heading to the west; there could be no doubt that her crew was in charge and taking her back to Yarmouth.

'That is the *Standard*,' he said tonelessly.

'Aye.' Fairfax spoke between clenched teeth. 'Our broadside will bear. We could fire into her.'

'We shall do no such thing, Captain Fairfax. Let her go.' Duncan was forcing himself to speak calmly. 'I have ships enough—'

'Sir!' Lieutenant Cleland, at the rail beside them, interrupted without ceremony. 'Another's making sail – it's *Belliqueux*. You can hear her cable coming in, sir.'

The Admiral drew in his breath sharply. It was incredible, and it was true. Far out in the thinning veil of sea-mist a second ship was slowly moving, following the first. So even Inglis, popular as he was, had not been able to hold his men in hand. Two 64-gun ships were leaving him 'to redress their grievances' (in the language of these mutineers) in port. Probably they would join the rebellious ships at the Nore. He made his stunned mind think clearly and coolly. The only action he could take short of opening fire on his own mutinous ships was to set sail for the Texel immediately, before there were any more defections; and the feeble easterly drift of air made that impossible.

'Neither *Russell* nor *Ganges* has yet joined, sir,' Fairfax said quietly.

Fairfax rarely allowed any feeling to show through his imperturbable manner, but now Duncan could detect the sympathy – even pity – in his tone. The two deserting ships were well away to westward and crowding on more sail. He could see the details more plainly because the mist was shredding away. That should mean a freshening breeze. Even as the thought crossed his mind a catspaw flawed the smooth surface close to *Venerable*, and he felt the cool touch of wind on his cheek. Sou'-sou'-east. He prayed that it might hold there and strengthen.

'Make the signal to weigh, Captain, if you please.'

While the orders rang on the flagship's decks and the seamen raced aloft to make sail, the Admiral watched his other ships with acute anxiety. They were obeying the signal; slowly, it was true, but the canvas was being unfurled from the yards and hauled taut. His spirits rose a little. *Venerable* was moving, gathering way, with the signals for course and order fluttering at her yardarm in the freshening wind. But – there was a flag soaring to the masthead of *Lion*. A red flag. And *Lion* was going about, her sails slatting, to steady on an opposite course to the one he had ordered. Not *Lion* only. *Repulse* was following her example. The sun, flooding suddenly through the remnants of the mist, gilded the white canvas as the following breeze filled it and urged them towards the English coast six leagues away. And now another ship was turning—

Fairfax, positively running, clattered across the quarterdeck to stand beside the Admiral. He said nothing. Silently they watched, while *Leopard* and *Ardent*, *Isis* and *Mon-*

*mouth*, came about in turn and headed after *Lion*'s red flag of rebellion. For minute after minute the two men stood at the rail tense and anxious, while the defecting squadron dwindled to westward. But no other ship turned from the flagship's course.

Fairfax broke the silence, hesitantly.

'*Glatton, Adamant, Agamemnon.* And ourselves.' He paused. 'We hold on, sir?'

'I believe you are aware of my orders, Captain,' said Duncan, and turned away.

He had never before snubbed his Flag Captain like that; but he had never before seethed with bitter fury as he was seething now. Whether his anger should be directed at a slothful Admiralty or at disloyal seamen was immaterial. He was being made to bear the burden of others' criminal thoughtlessness. With four ships of the line he was expected to repel a great invasion fleet. The wind was south-easterly now, and if it backed a point or two it would be fair for the Dutch to come out. He could only hold on with the remnant of his ships.

Menzies appeared at his side to announce that breakfast was ready in his cabin. He waved the steward aside impatiently. It was impossible to think of food at this moment. He watched the topsails of the mutineer ships gleam and dip out of sight beyond the western horizon. The sun rose in a clear sky patched with small white clouds; the wind, freshening yet more, flecked a sea of glorious blue with dazzling points of white. Fairfax had hoisted every inch of canvas the yards would carry, the other three ships were doing the same, and the squadron of four towering vessels dashing the spray from their bows as they leaned to the wind in their steady purposeful rush across the ungoverned sea was the epitome of the seaman's triumph. Adam Duncan felt his heart lift as he watched his three consorts holding their station on his lee quarter. *Adamant*, the smallest – she carried only fifty guns – was holding her own by virtue of perfectly trimmed sails; Hotham, in command, knew his business, and Onslow would be watching critically. Vice-Admiral Richard Onslow, who had hurriedly transferred to *Adamant* when his own ship mutinied, was a first-rate sailor.

A seaman trotted aft and struck four double clangs from the bell slung under the coving of the poop. Eight bells of the forenoon watch. If the wind held fair they should be off the Texel by daybreak tomorrow. The rage and despair had ebbed from the Admiral's mind and a rising flood of determination was fast replacing his gloom. His enterprise was now a desperate one; old as he was, he could begin to take a kind of pleasure in its very desperation.

An alteration in the squadron caught his eye. *Glatton* was out of station, falling away to leeward. He had opened his mouth to call Captain Fairfax's attention to it when he saw that Fairfax was already staring at *Glatton*. Something in the flag captain's rigid attitude startled him and he swung round again to gaze at the erring ship. *Glatton* was turning from her course – and *Agamemnon*, too, was going about. A small dark bundle rose jerkily to *Agamemnon*'s fore topgallant masthead and fluttered free. It was the red flag.

Silent, unmoving, the Admiral watched while the two ships completed their turn and dropped rapidly astern, headed for England. Then he straightened his big shoulders and set his back to them. Fairfax was facing him, staring blankly past him at the departing ships; so was Cleland, and Porteous, and the midshipman of the watch; so was Menzies, who had come up the quarterdeck ladder, doubtless to cajole him into eating something. With a faintly comical effect, their eyes all turned simultaneously to him.

'Captain Fairfax,' Duncan said briskly, 'I'd take a reef in the tops'ls, if I may suggest it. That will make it easier for *Adamant* to keep station.'

Fairfax gulped. 'Aye aye, sir.'

'I shall take some breakfast. Pray call me if the wind changes.'

The Admiral, punctiliously returning the salutes of his officers, followed Menzies below.

## III

The charcoal grey of first light paled slowly to the yellowish glimmer of an overcast dawn. The wind of dawn, gusty and changeable, ruffled the long slow waves that journeyed endlessly from the invisible coast of North Holland. Two dark shapes, one larger than the other, and three much smaller ones, lay rocking gently on the swell; the sloops *Garland* and *Stork* and the cutter *Rose* had joined Admiral Duncan's tiny squadron overnight, thereby providing it with eyes though not with increased fighting strength. A boat was creeping across from *Adamant* to *Venerable*.

The Admiral was on deck to receive Vice-Admiral Onslow and Captain Hotham of *Adamant* and lead them to his cabin. The smoky light of the oil-lamp showed the chart spread on the table and the three steaming mugs of coffee placed there by the efficient Menzies. The visitors threw off their boat-cloaks and sat down at the table, Hotham glancing a trifle nervously at the Vice-Admiral. Onslow was tall and thin, with heavy black eyebrows that contrasted sharply with his well-powdered hair; his somewhat cadaverous face wore a grave and resolute expression. He spoke incisively as soon as he was seated.

'With your leave, sir, I have to propose an immediate withdrawal while the wind holds fair.'

He paused and looked at Duncan, evidently expecting comment. The Admiral sipped his coffee and waited, his big face expressionless.

'While I applaud your courage, sir,' Onslow went on determinedly, 'I cannot but deprecate its uselessness. You have one ship of seventy-four guns, one of fifty. With the best will in the world you can't hope to effect anything against a fleet of forty which includes eighteen ships of the line. Moreover, there's every sign that the mutiny at home will attain the proportions of a revolution. A navy under the red flag won't allow two loyal ships to remain here unmolested. It's likely enough we'll have a squadron of force coming after us, in command of these Jacobin rogues from the Nore—'

'One moment, pray.' Duncan raised a hand apologetically. 'Your coffee will get cold – I fear my cabin is unduly draughty.'

The Vice-Admiral, scowling, took a gulp of coffee. When the choking occasioned by its scalding heat had subsided he continued his argument.

'Your best course, I submit, is to withdraw to Leith Roads. There these loyal ships would be secure both from the Texel and from the Nore – and could form the nucleus of a fleet to counter the rebellion. I urge this, sir, with the greatest sincerity and after long consideration. Captain Hotham, I believe, agrees with me.'

Duncan turned an inquiring regard on the captain of the

*Adamant,* who fingered his stock and looked uncomfortable.

'Well – er – it seems to me, sir, that the Vice-Admiral's contention is – er – very reasonable,' he admitted.

Duncan nodded. 'Indeed it would be, Captain, if his premises were correct.' He faced Onslow. 'But – forgive me, sir – I question all your premises. The uselessness, as you call it, of my present operation I'll discuss in a moment. For the future of the mutiny, I must inform you that in my opinion it has nothing whatever to do with revolution and that it will be over within a fortnight at most. The seamen are not Jacobins – they are men driven to a last resort in order to force Admiralty and Government to meet their proper obligations. I fancy I've had better opportunity to form this opinion than you have.'

'My own ship was one of the first to mutiny,' Onslow said, clenching his fist. 'I was forced to leave *Nassau,* put into a boat and set ashore—'

'But without violence, I understand?'

'They didn't lay a hand on me, it's true. But—'

'If they'd been Jacobins, sir, the first thing they'd have done was to string you up to the yardarm. There have been a hundred other incidents to prove that the seamen are determined to act with moderation.'

'Moderation!' Onslow muttered explosively; but the Admiral was speaking to Captain Hotham.

'There have been no further troubles on board *Adamant,* Captain?'

'Not the slightest sign of trouble, sir,' Hotham said eagerly. 'You'd think the hands were trying to show they were sorry for that business off Yarmouth, the way they work.'

'The same can be said of *Venerable*'s men, as I've observed for myself.' The Admiral took a drink of coffee, eyeing the Vice-Admiral over the rim of his mug. 'As for Leith Roads, sir, I dare not go there. It would be said that I was homesick and wanted to be near my wife.'

'You make a jest of it, sir.' Onslow drew himself up in a huff. 'I put the suggestion in all seriousness.'

'And in all seriousness I must decline it,' said Duncan equably. 'My orders are clear and I shall obey them to the letter. I am to prevent the Dutch invasion fleet from leaving the Texel and I shall do so.' He glanced at the chronometer on the bulkhead. 'The *Rose* cutter will have sailed to look into the Texel. As soon as I receive Lieutenant Brodie's report on the situation there I shall put my plan into action – a plan, gentlemen, which Captain Fairfax has approved. I anticipate your own approval when I have laid it before you, as I shall now proceed to do. – But your mugs are empty.'

He rang the small bell on his desk. The Vice-Admiral had not relaxed his scowl.

'And if, as you say, my – ah – premises are incorrect,' he said stubbornly. 'If you are right, sir, and the mutiny is to come to an end within a fortnight. The great and immediate danger remains – *Adamant* and *Venerable* alone face an enemy of at least ten times their strength. If it comes to a fight, what then?'

'If it comes to a fight,' Duncan repeated slowly, 'then, sir, I hope we shall do our duty. We shall engage the enemy. Captain Hotham, you will fight *Adamant* as long as you have a gun that will fire and a timber above water. *Venerable* will do the same. – Thank you, Menzies. More coffee, gentlemen. And now, pray consider the chart a moment.'

Onslow with frowning scepticism, Hotham with curiosity, followed the stabbings and outlinings of the Admiral's forefinger on the stiff paper. When Duncan sat back from the chart and began to detail the plan that had resulted from last night's sleepless hours they were ready to listen to him. Hotham's eyes sparkled, a grin spread across his face, and at last he burst out laughing. And by then a grim smile was perceptible on the Vice-Admiral's thin lips.

## IV

The cutter *Rose* came flying back on a fresh easterly breeze with the cloudy sunrise behind her. Lieutenant Brodie had taken her well within range of the forts, which had both opened fire on the impudent intruder (like trying to kill a moth with a musket, as Brodie said), and penetrated the entrance of the Texel almost within hail of the Dutch ships at the outermost moorings. Himself clinging to the single masthead of his tiny craft while she raced back and forth, he had brought back the information for which the Admiral waited – and more besides. A surprised Dutch fisherman had been snatched from his coble, questioned by one of

*Rose*'s crew who hailed originally from Terschelling, and restored to his boat unharmed. It was common knowledge on the shores of the Wieringer Meer, said this informant, that 80,000 French troops were at the Hague – some said already embarked in the forty merchant ships converted for use as transports. Brodie's own observations added that there were thirty ships of war (not counting frigates) in the Texel, and that of these seventeen were either 74's or 64's; all appeared to be manned and ready for sea.

At sunrise the wind had steadied, a fresh breeze from a little north of east. If the invasion fleet intended to sail today, they could have no more favourable wind. Duncan's plan required reasonably good visibility, and though the sky remained overcast there was no rain or sea-mist. He acted at once.

There could be no doubt that *Rose*'s daring foray would have alerted every lookout post along the Dutch coast in addition to the watchers on the battlements of the Texel forts. The advent of an English cutter to spy out the anchorage, after a period when there had been no *verdammt Engländers* to be seen, was enough to set all available eyes waching the westward sea. The watchers saw two ships of the line, one larger than the other, appear over the eastern horizon and beat slowly towards the coast. Soon a number of smaller craft could be made out; these kept well to seaward of the others. The line-of-battle ships turned southward when they were two miles offshore and passed slowly across the Texel entrance, the smaller vessel leading and displaying the pendant and red ensign of a Rear-Admiral of the Red. A signal hoist brought one of the small craft, a sloop, from her seaward station to remain beating up and down some three miles off the Texel while the others turned westward and disappeared again over the horizon. This was all for that day; but if the invasion fleet had thought to sail, it was enough to give them pause. What, they were asking themselves, lay beyond the western horizon?

Next morning two more ships came in sight – they could have been the same ships, but for the fact that the larger ship, in the lead, showed a blue ensign at the main. There were no smaller vessels with them this time. They cruised past in the same leisurely manner, keeping just out of range of the forts' batteries, and showed no disposition to retire beyond the horizon. At sunset they were still there, hove-to three or four miles from the coast. Were they waiting for the rest of a big fleet to come up? Or was this display of only two ships at a time a trailing of the coat, a decoy of some kind? As the sun dropped below the bars of cloud on the horizon these questions were being anxiously debated between the admirals and army commanders in the Texel anchorage.

Admiral Duncan could have supplied the answers. At sunset he was holding a final conference with Vice-Admiral Onslow before the latter's return to *Adamant*. The 50-gun ship made sail half-an-hour later and headed seaward into the gathering twilight. Duncan sent for his pilot.

'I propose to moor to the outer buoy of the Texel, Mr. Porteous,' he said. 'When can you find it for me?'

The Pilot's jaw dropped. 'The – the outer buoy, sir? But there's little enough water there even for these shallow-draught Dutchmen—'

'I'm aware of that, Mr. Porteous. We've taken soundings round that buoy before now – eh, Mr. Cleland?'

The First Lieutenant grinned a trifle sheepishly. There had been a lumpy sea when *Venerable*'s cutter had been sent away to take soundings, on the flagship's first visit two years ago, and Cleland had taken a ducking overboard as well as accurate soundings. Captain Fairfax, behind the Admiral, made a noise that could have been a chuckle.

'I recall Mr. Cleland found no bottom, sir,' he remarked.

'So you see, Mr. Porteous,' Duncan continued equably, 'I know what I'm doing. Can you find that buoy by night?'

'I – I doubt it, sir,' Porteous stammered. 'I very much doubt it.'

'Then we shall move inshore before dawn. Captain Fairfax, please to continue hove-to. Let the men get as much sleep as they can. I shall want them at quarters continuously, watch and watch, as long as *Venerable* remains at the outer buoy.'

'Aye aye, sir.'

'S-sir!' It was plainly fear that was making the Pilot bold enough to protest. 'The channel at the outer buoy is barely wide enough for one seventy-four to pass at a time, and the banks—'

'Precisely so, Mr. Porteous. That is the whole point.'

'B-but it's nearing springs, sir, and – and – and you could be sunk, sir, at that mooring.'

'Mr. Porteous,' said the Admiral with a hint of impatience in his deep voice, 'as you've just been told, I have the soundings to a fathom. I know that if they sink me my keel will be on the bottom and my flag still flying above the surface – and moreover, Mr. Porteous, the channel will be blocked. Do you desire any further explanation?'

The Pilot glanced quickly at Fairfax and Cleland and saw them smiling. He ran a finger round his neck inside his stock.

'N-no, sir. Thank you, sir.'

'Then I rely on you to do your duty, which is to bring this ship to the outer buoy at first light tomorrow morning.'

It was again a cloudy morning, this time with a drift of haze blowing off the land. The leadsman was in the chains as *Venerable*, close hauled, edged through the shifting glimmer of a choppy sea under a sky that paled slowly and reluctantly with the dawn. The flagship was already so close to the land that the line of dunes on the Helder shore could be seen even through the haze. Porteous, peering from binnacle to coast, muttered to the quartermaster to bear up a trifle, and the Admiral turned sharply at the sound of his voice.

'Well, Mr. Porteous?'

'We're within a half-mile of it, sir. And this course is right.' Porteous paused to listen to the chant of the leadsman. 'So are the soundings, sir,' he added.

Duncan glanced for'ard along the deck where a party was lugging a cable aft to pass it through a gunport on the starboard side. On the fo'c'sle head Cleland was directing the casting-loose of the anchor lashings. *Venerable* clawed her slow way onward towards the shore under reefed topsails for five minutes more. Then the lookout hailed from the foremast crosstrees.

'Object fine on th' labb'd bow! A buoy, sir!'

The Admiral turned to nod benevolently at Porteous, whose expression was a curious mingling of satisfaction and dismay.

The buoy was a massive cube made of great baulks of timber bolted together. When the flagship, under Fairfax's careful seamanship, had crept to within a third of a cable's length and brought the buoy on her starboard beam, the anchor was let go. As the cable roared out, the longboat plumped into the water and came alongside below the after gunport to receive the second cable, which was coiled down into her sternsheets. In fifteen minutes this 'spring' had been rove through the huge iron ring on the buoy and the bight brought back aboard. With the easterly breeze pushing her to seaward, and adjustable points of attachment fore and aft, *Venerable* could now bring her broadside to bear on the Texel entrance or on any point within ten degrees to north or south of it.

'Hoist away, Captain,' Duncan ordered; and a string of bunting went fluttering up to the yardarm.

That was the first of many hoists. The watchers on the Texel and Helder forts observed them with anxiety and much speculation. As soon as the morning haze cleared they had perceived the situation. An enemy 74 had actually moored at the outer buoy (unhappily it was a short quarter-mile beyond the extreme range of their eighteen-pounders) and another enemy ship was hove-to on the horizon. Every signal made by the nearer ship was exactly repeated by the other; it was perfectly obvious that the signals were being relayed to a ship or fleet out of sight below the horizon. And it was very soon made plain that there was a fleet there – the signals were preceded by numeral pendants, showing that they were addressed to different ships. The wind might continue to stand fair for England, but the invasion fleet dared not sail in the face of such a threat.

So for three days and three nights *Venerable* stayed at the outer buoy of the Texel, signalling endlessly by day to a non-existent fleet and by night rowing continuous guard; for a cutting-out expedition was the Admiral's nightly fear. There was little sleep for anyone on board during that period. Duncan himself lay awake for long hours, too keenly aware of the thread by which hung his fate, and the fate of England, to sleep. He was masquerading as an Apollyon straddling right across the way, while he was in fact as harmless as the two chained lions that needlessly affrighted the Pilgrim. De Winter had only to doubt, to send a testing force of two or three ships of the line, and it would be revealed that Duncan had no more than the 50-gun *Adamant* to summon to his aid. In these wakeful hours Adam Duncan prayed. He could not keep himself from thinking that this was a test of his faith. And – if indeed this was such a test – he found his faith rewarded.

In the afternoon of June 5th two ships of the line beat up

from westward. They were *Sanspareil* and *Russell*, both under command and with urgent orders from Earl Spencer to join the Texel squadron. Captain Trollope of the *Russell* came on board the flagship with the news that the Nore mutiny was nearing a climax; the rebel ships had attempted to blockade the Port of London, and as a defensive measure all the Thames buoys, marks, and navigational aids had been removed or destroyed. But the Admiral's worst trial was at an end. Two days later Rear-Admiral Sir Roger Curtis joined him with six line-of-battle ships. And now the wind might blow easterly for ever if it wished, and bring out the great invasion fleet of the French and Batavian Republics; Admiral Duncan was ready for it.

It was June 16th when the frigate *Circe* (whose incipient mutiny the admirable Halkett had put down without any violence) arrived off the Texel with the First Lord's letter, dated two days earlier.

Spencer took pleasure in 'announcing the approaching termination of the Mutiny at the Nore in as desirable a manner as could under all the circumstances be wished'. The rebel ships had all submitted at discretion. *Sandwich*, the 'flagship' of the mutineer's leader Richard Parker, had run into harbour and rendered up Parker and his associates. Parker and the ringleaders to the number of twenty or thirty would doubtless be hanged, but the rest of the mutineers – sixteen thousand men or more – would be freely pardoned, except about 180 men guilty of violence towards their helpless officers, who would be sent to the hulks.

It was as satisfactory as Adam Duncan could have hoped. Except for those 180 men. He promised himself that he would press for their freedom – but it must take second place in his desires now. Until the threat of invasion from Holland was removed once for all that must be his sole concern. There was still a chance that the Dutch would come out.

So he and his ships had remained on their station thereafter, week after week, month after month, until the absolute need of replacing broken spars and caulking leaky timbers had driven him back to Yarmouth at the end of September.

Within ten days he was taking the familiar sea road again. The Dutch were out at last.

# SEVEN

## I

The old man stood by the rail of the flagship's stern gallery, watching the sea miles flowing away into the gathering twilight. *Venerable*'s wake foamed boldly white from her massive quarters and creaking rudder, then spread as it fell astern across the grey North Sea waves, diffusing, fading, lost far away in the windy brume of evening. Irrevocably lost, irrevocably past. Merged in the ocean it had stirred and marked for a few short minutes. That was the life of man – a scratch on the face of eternal waters, effaced for ever almost as soon as it was made. Duncan smiled faintly at his thought, because it was so commonplace and he had so often entertained it. It had been with him, indeed, throughout these two days, since he had sailed from Yarmouth; though (now he came to consider it) the memories of his own life that had risen before him during the voyage had not been in the least faded or diffuse. He had noticed lately how increasingly clear his recollection of past events was growing, even when the events had taken place half a century ago. His father the Provost had revealed this same increasing intimacy with the past, he remembered, a few years before his death. It was an old man's gift.

He shook his massive head as if to free himself from the mesmeric effect of that receding wake. If the past must always drop astern, the future still lay ahead, and *Venerable*'s streaming wake meant that she was bearing him towards the culmination of his life, the thing for which Providence had armed and guided him. He saw the flagship's track now as a road made plain in the wilderness. The tortuous sea-lanes that had taken him across the world and back, the byways bright or sombre along which he had stumbled through the years, had all the time been leading him to this last purposeful sea road. Suddenly he was certain that the road led straight to his objective, the long-delayed meeting with the Dutch Fleet. That meeting might end in triumph or defeat; for himself, in death or in life and fame. Providence had arranged all that. It was enough for Adam Duncan to be sure of the encounter.

## II

He paced the sheltered length of the stern gallery, stooping so that his head would clear the projecting poop beams above him. The walk towards the big carved Neptune at the larboard end of the gallery was only slightly uphill, because with this light quartering wind *Venerable*'s list was inconsiderable. The wind was very little east of north and tending to back. If it backed through north to nor'-nor'-west it was likely to become stronger and squally; blowing straight on to the Dutch coast which lay five leagues away. At present his ships were carrying all plain sail to the top-gallants. As he paced up and down he could see four of them only, for the protecting Neptunes at the ends of the gallery cut off his view, but he knew there were thirteen in company now, each keeping her station on the flagship. It could be a sign of Providence's benevolent intentions that the two ships he had left refitting at Yarmouth had made the Texel rendezvous just as he was leaving it. When *Russell* and *Adamant* were found, as he was confident they would be, he would have sixteen of the line, the same number as De Winter, according to report. An even match, on the face of it – but the steady clank of *Venerable*'s pumps was being echoed aboard the majority of his weatherbeaten ships, and in half of them at least the mast and spars were long over-due for replacement. The balance of strength, he thought, was probably restored by the fact that the Dutch seamen had not been as constantly at sea as his own men; all the courage and confidence in the world – and the Dutch had never been defeated at sea – could hardly compensate for lack of regular exercise in the manifold skills required of a fighting seaman.

All in all, then, the two fleets would be as equal in force as any that had ever met in battle. There was one thing, though, that was an unknown quantity, and it could prove the deciding factor: the desire of the British seamen to wipe out the disgrace of the late mutiny. If that was indeed the common feeling throughout his Fleet—

'By'r leave, sir.'

In his preoccupied walking up and down he had almost

passed by Fairfax, who was standing in the doorway of the gallery with his hat in his hand.

'Well, Captain?' said Duncan, halting.

'Orders for the night, sir,' Fairfax said with a slight hesitation. 'You said you were turning in early.'

'Of course, of course.' His meditations had made him forget the passage of time. 'I've no special order, Captain – except that I'm to be called at once if there's any news of the Dutch.'

'Aye aye, sir.'

'You've doubled the lookouts?'

'Yes, sir. Main and fore.'

'Please to have them relieved every two hours, Captain. A man's eyes tire quickly and we don't want De Winter to slip past us in the dark.'

The Admiral paused to reflect. His present course was based on probabilities. Whatever De Winter's reason for putting to sea, it could hardly be a direct invasion, since there were no transports with him. He would be aware that a British fleet would seek action, and he would either position himself to accept it or try to return to the Texel. In either of these cases he would not go far to the westward or far from his own coast, so that the chances were that he would be found, sooner or later, between Duncan's ships and the coast of Holland.

'What is our speed?' he demanded, emerging suddenly from his reverie.

'Six knots, sir. Wind'll freshen, I fancy.'

'Yes.'

It had been four in the afternoon when he had boarded *Venerable* after his excursion in *Circe*. Since then the Fleet had made a slow progress southward down the Dutch coast, with frequent reconnaissances coastward by *Circe* and the cutters. During the night they could make another sixty miles of southing. If they were to come up with De Winter at all, it would be well before tomorrow noon; and if his assessment of the probabilities were correct, the likelihood was that he would sight *Russell* or *Adamant* soon after daybreak.

'Captain Fairfax,' he said with unusual earnestness, 'I desire you'll give your personal attention to this. Breakfast for the watch below is to be served at four bells of the morning watch and for the watch on deck immediately afterwards. It's to be a good breakfast, the best the cooks can muster – and every man is to eat his fill. I would suggest that an officer, Mr. Clay for instance, should give an eye to the food.'

'I'd prefer to make the rounds myself, sir.'

'Very well, Captain. Then that is all – except that I have every expectation of meeting the Dutch fleet early in the forenoon. I shall be on deck at first light.'

'Aye aye, sir.'

Fairfax rammed his hat on his head, touched its brim, and departed. The Admiral turned for a last glance over the dark waste of sea astern. The sun had dipped unseen below the horizon, hidden by the drifts of twilight cloud; but through a transient gap low on the western rim a faint remembrance of sunset glowed and faded. For a few seconds the tumbling ridges of the waves gave back its blood-red hue.

## III

Admiral Duncan came on deck a little before dawn in the morning of Wednesday October 12th, after as good a night's sleep as he had ever had in his life. *Venerable* was snoring along at seven knots through a short and lumpy sea, and he noticed at once that the wind had backed west of north. Already there was light enough to make out the ships in company – the six ships astern of the flagship in tolerable line, *Monarch* on her starboard beam leading the seven ships of the weather division. Onslow's flagship, like *Venerable,* had taken in her top-gallant sails; that was because five at least of the others were incapable of keeping up with them. Duncan frowned as this recalled one of his problems. Ideally, for the engagements in line of battle each ship should engage her opponent in the enemy line at the same instant, which meant keeping rigid station until the actual moment of engagement; with a fleet of uneven sailers such as this an Admiral would have great difficulty in even approaching the ideal. Two or three ships engaging a well stationed line-of-battle ten minutes in advance of their companions could be pounded to splinters before support reached them.

Captain Fairfax, approaching to bid him good morning, exorcized this doleful vision for a moment. He returned the

Flag Captain's greeting cheerfully, and Fairfax moved away to join the group of dark figures near the lee quarterdeck rail. There had been no need for further conversation. If there had been anything to report Fairfax would have reported it; and there was no point in repeating what he already knew – that the Admiral would take full command, of the flagship as well as of the Fleet, from the moment the enemy was sighted. Duncan went to the empty deck space by the weather rail and began his morning walk up and down.

There was of course one possibility which would make the strict maintenance of his battle line less important: if he broke the enemy line with two divisions the inevitable slight confusion would give no advantage to the Dutch, whose own line would lose its strength. But that manœuvre, he had resolved, must remain only a possibility. The tactics of John Clerk of Eldin might be effective, but Providence should decide whether Adam Duncan was to be the first seaman to put them to the proof. Providence, he was assured, would give him a sufficient sign.

The ragged clouds in the east were showing a pallor like the gleam of a fish's belly. Dawn was here. There were seven or eight officers on the quarterdeck this morning, he noticed now – more than usual – and the undercurrent of excitement in the murmur of subdued conversation that came to his ears roused an answering thrill in himself. As he turned in his pacing he saw that the small figure on the fringe of the group was Midshipman Stewart. Stewart was thirteen years old. If his Admiral could feel a thrill of excitement at sixty-six, what must young Stewart be feeling, with a great battle – perhaps the most important sea-fight in England's history – in prospect? He caught himself up there. Was he overrating the vital significance of the coming struggle? He thought not. If the Dutch defeated him, destroyed his Fleet, England's hopes of opposing the growing tyranny of France were gone. If he destroyed De Winter's ships the greatest threat of all, the threat to an England ill-prepared and poor in spirit, would be removed for ever. The war against Jacobinism would go on; there would be other great battles, sea-fights perhaps more famous in history than this; but it would be his victory that gave the impetus for a final triumph, that showed the world – and England herself – that England could rise above her corruption and self-seeking and stand forth as the last champion of liberty.

The Admiral's unwontedly exalted thoughts were interrupted by a faint squeal and a guffaw from below decks for'ard. It had been a feminine squeal. There were two dozen women on board, the 'wives' of seamen. Some of them were doubtless legally married, but it was sufficient for a woman to declare herself a man's wife to gain admission to the fo'c'sle. Duncan had an inherent dislike of a system which undoubtedly condoned promiscuity, and was able to tolerate it only by telling himself that no woman would face the squalor of a fo'c'sle, let alone the horrors of the 'tween-decks during a battle, if she did not love her man as truly as the best of wives. All the same, he had had all of them except two dozen bundled ashore before he sailed for the Texel; those who remained could be useful in assisting the surgeon's mates, and there was not room for more to live on board with any kind of decency. Henrietta would throw up her hands in dismay if she could see the conditions they lived in. Henrietta—

'Deck, there! Two sail, labb'd beam!'

The masthead hail brought the Admiral to a full halt. At the larboard rail every officer had turned to stare to landward, and those who had telescopes were peering eagerly through them as if they expected to catch sight of ships that must be as yet hull-down even from the masthead.

'Mr. Clay,' began Fairfax, and Clay was racing up the mizzen shrouds before he could complete the order.

The quarterdeck was tensely silent until Clay came swarming down again. Duncan and Fairfax moved to meet him.

'*Russell* and *Adamant*, sir – not a doubt of it.' Clay, panting, addressed himself to the Admiral. 'Not light enough yet to make out if they're signalling.' He gulped for breath. 'But *Circe*'s heading for the Fleet, sir – we'll know in a minute.'

The October daybreak, diffusing grey light sullenly through the clouds that scudded southward over the mastheads, showed a dark sea veiled here and there with drifting rain-squalls. But the eastern horizon was clear, and the tiny triangle of the frigate's sails was lifting on its black line a very few minutes after Clay had made his report. As Duncan went to the larboard rail the cluster of officers fell back to give him space.

*Circe* was hull-up now, racing with her news as fast as she had raced yesterday off the Texel, yet it seemed an unconscionable time before she was close enough for there to be any hope of reading a signal.

'Mr. Stewart!'

But Midshipman Stewart was waiting at his elbow. The telescope he raised was trembling with his excitement, but he seemed to know his signal-book by heart.

' "Enemy in s-sight," s-sir.' His voice, newly broken, squeaked excruciatingly. ' "S-sixteen sail of the line," sir.'

He lowered the telescope, and then raised it again quickly. Duncan's own keen sight had seen the hoist come fluttering down and another take its place.

' "Request to speak the Admiral," sir,' Stewart read off.

'Very well, Mr. Stewart. Make *Circe*'s pendant and "Come within hail," if you please. As soon as she acknowledges, hoist the General pendant and make Number Ten.'

By now *Circe*'s signal would have been read on the quarterdecks of most of his Fleet, but he could imagine the bustle of excitement among the seamen – instantly to be converted into strenuous action – when they saw Number 10 fluttering from the Admiral's yardarm. Every seaman of experience among them would recognize the signal *Prepare for Battle.* On board the flagship, Fairfax had chosen to interpret his order to Stewart as an order to himself. He snapped three words; Cleland leaped down the quarterdeck ladder, bellowing as he went; Clay and Douglas sprang shouting after him and Major Trollope, his red coat glowing in the increasing light, stumped to the rail to bark loudly at a sentry below him. In a moment the ship was a reverberating wooden shell full of noise – drums beating, whistles shrilling, mallets thudding below decks, horny feet making their curious muffled thunder as the hands poured up on deck. The galley fire was being doused, bulkheads knocked down, hammocks dragged to the bulwarks to be lashed there as protection against flying splinters and the bullets from the enemy's fighting-tops. It was in the midst of this hubbub that *Circe* came foaming up, to back her topsails and hail the flagship. Halkett's voice pierced the tumult. The Dutch Fleet was seven miles distant, bearing south-south-west and steering to northward. Three admirals' flags. Sixteen of the line and five frigates. Duncan took Fairfax's speaking-trumpet and replied himself.

'Thank you, Mr. Halkett. Take station to windward of the weather division, if you please.'

Halkett waved his hat. The frigate paid off, filled on the larboard tack, and sped astern of *Venerable*. Douglas, the third lieutenant, was waiting at the Admiral's side when he turned. Masthead lookout reported *Russell* hull-up and heading for the Fleet, with *Adamant* in company.

'Thank you, Mr. Douglas. Mr. Stewart! Make "Close with the Admiral" to *Russell*, if you please.'

Stewart had Midshipman Prothero to help him now, which was just as well; the mass of bunting – numeral flags, alphabeticals, special pendants – needed careful handling at the signal locker, and the yardarm halyards which two seamen were operating were in continual danger of fouling the great square of netting now being hauled taut overhead. Half-a-dozen hands were securing the netting to mizzen and main shrouds, a canopy of rope above the after deck to trap the blocks and shattered spars which might fall from aloft under enemy fire, a danger almost as great as the balls themselves. It was the most immediate reminder of what was now certain to come, and despite his outward imperturbability Duncan felt the queer lift of something inside his upper chest just as he had felt it half a century ago, when he was a boy with his first enemy action impending. For some reason the phrase 'second childhood' flitted across his mind, and his lips twitched at the absurd train of thought it suggested.

He became aware of the strange silence around him. Fairfax came stumping across the quarterdeck, the *clap-clap* of his buckled shoes sounding loud in the stillness.

'Cleared for action, sir.'

'Very good, Captain.'

Duncan glanced for'ard along the deck. The scrubbed planking, where a few moments ago a milling crowd of seamen had surged in apparent chaos, looked almost empty. On either hand the trim alignment of cannon diminished in perspective, the guns on their wooden-wheeled trucks nuzzling the closed gunports, and by each gun stood its crew of six men – not rigid at attention like the marines but still and alert. Major Trollope's men made a brilliant splash of colour amidships, drawn up in double ranks just for'ard of the mainmast with Trollope stiff as a scarlet image in front of them. The tall cylindrical hats of the marines, with loops of gold braid round them, looked like a row of decorated chimney-pots. Clay and Douglas, in charge of the after and for'ard guns respectively, seemed to be imitating the rigidity of the major of marines as they stood facing aft, comparatively drab in their dark coats and big cocked hats. Behind Fairfax on the quarterdeck Cleland and Paterson and the pilot, Porteous, were standing equally motionless. The boyish apprehension Duncan had felt was superseded by a thrill of pride – and then, almost instantly, a wave of sadness flooded over him. How many of these men, most of them less than half his age, would be still alive by nightfall? How many of them maimed or disfigured for life?

A thin veil of rain drew across the deck and its chill touch on his face wiped the untimely thought from his mind. An old man's sentimentality was not for an Admiral about to engage a fleet that had never been beaten.

'Dismiss the watch below, Captain Fairfax, if you please.'

There was no point in keeping men at quarters in these brief but chilling rain squalls. It would be an hour at the very least before De Winter's ships were hull-up.

'Mr. Stewart, make the General signal and "Form line on starboard bearing". Square away, Captain.'

He found a moment to enjoy the half-forgotten sensation of absolute command again. Hitherto he had been in some sense a passenger, a personage of importance indeed but rather as a controller than as a commander. Now he had direct command of *Venerable* as well as of the Fleet. When the moment of engagement came and every captain must fight his ship as he found best, it would be Adam Duncan who fought *Venerable*.

The flagship was heeling slightly as she began to move through the water. Out to starboard the ships of the weather division were turning with stately slowness into line. He looked up at the long command pendant streaming in the wind, conjured into his mind's eye the familiar pattern of the chart.

'Course sou'-sou'-east, Captain. Mr. Stewart, make that course to the Fleet.'

Beneath the cloudy sky the sails of *Russell* and the smaller *Adamant* were clear-cut white as they stood in to follow the rear ships of Onslow's division. Duncan pulled out his watch. It was thirty-eight minutes past nine – three-quarters of an hour since *Circe* had been sighted. What had De Winter done in that time? With this wind blowing onshore he could be making towards the coast, over the shoals where he could not be followed—

'Mr. Stewart! General pendant and "Make more sail". – I'll have those topgallants on her, Captain, if you please.'

*Isis* and *Lancaster, Beaulieu* and *Belliqueux* – those were four of the slower ships. They would have to keep up as best they could. He couldn't risk De Winter's evading him because of his tardiness in attacking. The rain-squall had blown clear again, but his blue coat was wet – his second-best coat, he remembered, with the split beneath the arm-pit that Henrietta had mended so neatly four days ago in Yarmouth. For the coming engagement, he supposed, he had better put on his silk stockings and the best coat with all that heavy gold braid on cuffs and collar and lapels. There was ample time to do that.

'Will you take over the deck, Captain? I'm going below for a few minutes.'

The Admiral's steward was coming out of his cabin as he reached it. Menzies's craggy face wore a preoccupied expression and his thin lips were sucked in, giving him the look of the old woman who used to sell mussels in Dundee market when Duncan was a child. He remembered a visiting Vice-Admiral once remarking that 'there was a good wife lost in Menzies'.

'I've gie'd your cabin a tidy, sir,' Menzies said; his austere glance implied that the Admiral had left it in a mess. 'The coffee's hot. I'll bring ye a mug.'

'I have no time for coffee,' declared Duncan.

Menzies, stalking away, gave no sign that he had heard.

*Venerable* had been built for a flagship long ago, before the Admiralty had begun to question whether a ship's fighting efficiency was not more important than an Admiral's comfort, so there had been no knocking-down of bulkheads in his day cabin; Burnet would use it as an office during the battle, the Secretary's own cabin being in reserve for wounded officers. Menzies had cleared his desk and the top of his bookshelves and put all loose articles in the locked drawer beneath it (Duncan unlocked the drawer for a final glance at Henrietta's portrait) as some protection against the violence to come. The books had been secured with a device of Menzies's own – a neat strip of wood wedged in battens across the row of spines so that they could not fall out. As Duncan shrugged himself into his best uniform coat he noticed that they had been rearranged; it would be like Menzies to give all his books a good dusting just before a sea-fight. His Bible, he saw, had come to rest next to Clerk's *Essay on Naval Tactics*. Was there, perhaps, a 'sign' in that coincidence? He dismissed the thought.

'Coffee, sir,' said Menzies, coming in with a steaming mug.

'Thank you.'

'I've put out the new braided hat, sir, with the silk lining. It's on the chair yonder.'

Duncan smiled at him as he lifted the mug. 'I'm very fortunate, James, in having you to look after me.'

The steward cleared his throat and drew breath as if to speak, but the only result was a convulsive movement of his enormous adam's-apple. After a short but embarrassing pause he bent forward, flicked an invisible speck of dust from the Admiral's gold-braided sleeve, and then hurried out of the cabin.

Duncan buckled on his sword in its black scabbard. With the new silk-lined hat in his hand he took a quick glance round the cabin; he would not leave the deck again until the issue of the fight was decided – unless, of course, they had to carry him below. His eye fell on a patch of damp at the bottom of the bulkhead in the corner. Next time he was in Yarmouth the dockyard should make good that caulking or he'd know the reason why. Odd how his mind chose to occupy itself with small things instead of concentrating on the coming battle, now considering whether there was a trifle too much sugar in the coffee and now debating the propriety of discarding his hat (which was sure to irk his forehead) when the firing began. It was as though some inner man was urging him to stay here in this familiar retreat with his books and his thoughts, telling him that at sixty-six trivialities such as these were fitter mental pabulum than the problem of how to destroy an enemy fleet. The fingers of the clock on the bulkhead flicked all idle considerations from him as soon as he noticed them; they pointed to five minutes to ten. The Admiral closed the cabin door behind him, jammed his uncomfortable hat on his head, and went on deck.

The wind had backed still more. It was blowing from the north-west, straight on to the Dutch coast. His first glance was for *Venerable*'s sails; as he had expected, the careful Fairfax had trimmed them to the change of wind. His second glance was for the ships to starboard and astern, and at once he saw that his forebodings were justified. *Isis* and *Lancaster* of his own division had already fallen astern of their stations – there was at least three cable's-lengths between *Isis* and her next ahead, *Belliqueux*, who was herself too far behind *Bedford*.

'Mr. Stewart! Number Sixty-Seven to *Iis* and *Lancaster*.'

'Aye aye, sir.'

Midshipman Stewart's thin face was very pale and his eyes were very bright. He jumped for the signal locker with tremendous alacrity, as though he was glad of having something to do. Stewart was less than a year older than his son Robert, Duncan remembered, and recalled his own youthful agonies during this trying period of waiting before an engagement. To give Stewart work to occupy him was a kindness; and there was no need to look for excuses. *Russel* was swinging away to larboard and had to be called to order. *Isis* was still not making all the sail she should. The pendants and signal flags went swinging up to his yardarm every minute. And all the time those on the quarterdeck, including the Admiral himself, had an ear cocked eagerly for the hail from the masthead. That the enemy was there, just over the horizon, they knew well enough: but to sight them from *Venerable* herself was somehow different, clinching the matter beyond the shadow of doubt.

The hail came ten minutes after the Admiral's return to the quarterdeck.

'De-e-ck! Fleet in sight – it's the Dutch, sir!'

The First Lieutenant, his dark eyes shining, had placed himself where Duncan would see him when he turned. At the Admiral's nod he was away, climbing like a cat to the masthead, and was back on deck with a speed which the most agile topman could hardly have equalled.

'Sixteen sail, sir, in close line heading north-east. Broad on our starboard bow – I'd say sou'-sou'-west.'

So the south-easterly course was bringing the British ships to a point on De Winter's course well ahead of the

Dutch. He did not want to await the Dutch admiral and give him a chance to manoeuvre.

'We shall alter course, Captain. Due south. Mr. Stewart, make the General pendant and "Steer south", if you please.'

The double line of ships made the slight turn, their wakes creaming on the grey chop of the waves. Like pale ghosts, the rain-squalls hung on the southern horizon, baffling the telescopes that were trained continuously on the straight dark rim whenever it appeared. There was a grunt from Fairfax, and simultaneously the hazy circle of Duncan's glass brought up the line of black specks, evenly spaced and close together like the posts of a distance fence. De Winter's ships.

Duncan was quite unaware of the great sigh that escaped him, and it was lost in the loud murmur of excitement and satisfaction from his officers. At last he was in sight of his goal.

## IV

It was a quarter past ten when the flagship's Number One gun, larboard side, fired its two alerting shots to call attention to the flags at the Admiral's yardarm: the General pendant, and Number Seven – 'general chase'. This was an invariable procedure in the circumstances. Though it was unlikely in the extreme that any of the ships of the line were ignorant of the Dutch fleet's presence close ahead, the *Vestal* and *Active* cutters. speeding like greyhounds beside the taller ships, could not yet have sighted the enemy. Moreover, the signal with its two-gun emphasis made it plain to every man in the Fleet that the Admiral intended a direct attack. But if Duncan's doubts of an engagement were now finally at an end, his anxieties were by no means over. An hour at the very least must elapse before he could bring his Fleet to close action with the enemy, and in that time he had to dispose his ships to the best possible advantage. The order of battle was prearranged, and every captain knew what station his ship had to take in the single line; but with vessels of uneven speed, in gusty weather with isolated squalls that sometimes urged the leading ships faster while those in the rear were feeling a lighter wind, it was an almost impossible task to maintain the proper intervals.

*Beaulieu* and *Belliqueux* were lagging, and *Venerable*'s repeated signals to make more sail produced little result.

The Admiral was eyeing the straining topgallant sails of the flagship with a meditative frown when the hail of 'Land in sight!' came from the masthead. Captain Fairfax came to stand beside him.

'They must be close inshore, sir,' Fairfax said.

That he should have ventured so obvious a statement showed his anxiety. Duncan nodded, his grey eyes narrowing. In De Winter's place he would have done the same. With a fleet of shallow-draught vessels, and five miles of shoal water under his lee, he would hug the nine-fathom line as closely as he dared, ready to turn coastward and draw the attacking ships into soundings where they would ground and lie at the mercy of the Dutch ships, who could still manoeuvre and pound them to pieces. He could not afford to take in topgallant sails; it was essential to strike at speed, to engage ship-to-ship before the Dutch had time to effect any such tactics.

A seaman came trotting aft to the bell under the quarterdeck rail and swung the clapper. Three double clangs. Six bells of the forenoon watch – eleven o'clock. The sense of urgency, of Time inexorably whirling him towards catastrophe because of something left undone, gripped him suddenly. But what more could he do? In the opalescent round of his telescope De Winter's ships were hull-up now, five miles away at most. Some of them were painted yellow, some black, but they were in taut line and stripped to topsails only. In less than an hour he had to oppose to that challenging rank a line-of-battle equally taut.

With an abruptness very unusual in him he swung round to face the Flag Captain.

'Turn up all hands, Captain.'

'Aye aye, sir.' Fairfax hesitated. 'Shall I beat to quarters, sir?'

'No. I want them mustered aft. And every officer on the quarterdeck.'

The boatswains' whistles shrilled, the hatchways vomited streams of men. In a minute and a half the deck space aft of the mainmast was packed with seamen and Trollope's marines were in rigid rank below the for'ard quarterdeck rail. Officers and midshipmen were grouped by the taffrail, some of them looking puzzled. Darby the chaplain was with them; but this was not an occasion for Darby's feeble utterances. The Admiral strode to the head of the quarterdeck ladder and took off his hat. His great voice easily dominated the noises of wind and waves.

'Let us pray!'

The momentary sibilance of surprise on the crowded deck died into silence.

'Lord God of Hosts, every man of us is about to place himself in Thy hands. Be with us in life and in death. In victory, if it be Thy will. Amen.' He paused for several seconds before clapping his hat on his head and turning briskly to Fairfax. 'Beat to quarters, Captain, if you please.'

For that short space of time the ship alone had seemed a living creature, with all her crew turned to stone. Now her human masters woke again to noise and action. The *rafale* of the drums, the bellowing of orders, the surge of swift and orderly movement, succeeded the silence like the breaking of a spell. The stream of seamen flowed for'ard along the deck, thinning rapidly as the gun-crews broke off to stand by their guns. The main body of the marines came clumping up the quarterdeck ladder to form along the rail at either hand, while a dozen of their company mounted the shrouds of fore and main and mizzen masts to take station in the tops, four to a mast.

'I'll have the guns loaded and run out now, Captain.'

The thrill of that ominous thunder could still stir him, Duncan found. There was no other sound so aptly suited to its implications. The rumble of the gun-trucks ceased, the last man scurried into stillness at his action station, the deck was quiet again except for the unending chord of the wind in the rigging and the rhythmic thud of *Venerable*'s pumps, which had been restarted. The flagship was as ready as she could be for the battle; the Admiral was not. He was frowning heavily as he told Stewart to prepare the special pendants of all sixteen ships for hoisting. In the few seconds of silence after his public prayer he had asked for guidance, but none had been given him nor had the sign he looked for appeared. His resolve still held – not to make the rash experiment advised by Clerk of Eldin unless Providence indicated it.

'General pendant and Number Ninety-five, Mr. Stewart. Hoist away.'

Up fluttered the coloured bunting with its order for each

ship to take station in the line as her particular pendant was thrown out. Duncan moved across the quarterdeck to watch the effect, and his heart sank. Not only were four of his ships badly out of station, but several of them were also out of sight – at the very moment of his order the Fleet had entered an area of small isolated rain-squalls, and the rear-most vessels were hidden behind grey curtains of falling rain.

He turned quickly to stare at the Dutch fleet. It was a shock to discover how close it was now, that long line of black or yellow ships moving in stately procession across his starboard bow. With his unaided eye he could make out the black dots of the open gunports and the large flags at the sterns and mastheads of the three ships which carried admirals. The telescope showed him a red flag, with a white quarter next to the staff, crowning the maintopmast of the fifth ship in the line – De Winter's flag. It showed him, too, the yellowish tinge of the waves through which the Dutch vessels moved.

'Sir!'

It was the Pilot, at his side. Porteous (perhaps remembering that evening off the Texel seven months ago) had his emotions in hand, but there was no mistaking the anxiety in his eyes.

'Well, Mr. Porteous?'

Porteous took a deep breath. 'By my reckoning, sir, the Dutch ships are well inside the nine-fathom line of soundings.'

'Yes?'

'I feel it's my duty to point this out, sir.' The Pilot was making himself speak firmly, as one having authority. 'I know the shoals here. A mile farther inshore, probably less, there's not depth enough for the seventy-fours of this Fleet. And the wind's onshore. They might draw off, sir, as the action begins, and put our ships aground.'

It was his own half-acknowledged fear. Voiced by another man, and that man the best of the North Sea pilots, it had greater force.

'As it's too late now, sir, to get between them and the land—'

Porteous broke off short and fell back a step. The Admiral's big fist had smitten with startling violence into the Admiral's open palm, and his stentorian bellow made the signal midshipman jump.

'Mr. Stewart! Haul down – and hoist the "Countermand"! Look lively, now!'

*To get between them and the land* – he must have been blind not to perceive the plain solution. As if the interference of the elements with his last signal had not been sign enough, it had needed John Porteous to act as the voice of Providence. Too late, as Porteous had said, to lead his battle line between the enemy and the land, but not too late for the tactics of Clerk of Eldin.

'Make General, Mr. Stewart, and Number Thirty-four.'

His sixteen ships were by now in considerable confusion, some making for their station in single line, others who had not seen the signal still holding on in the weather division. But the squalls had passed, and there was *Monarch* acknowledging No. 34, 'Pass through the enemy's line and engage them to leeward.' Onslow would know precisely what that implied – the attack in two divisions, breaking the line, holding the Dutch with an intensity of fire that would allow no manoeuvring to leeward. Confidence rose in him as he watched *Monarch* bear away with her attendant ships, under all plain sail with one reef in her topsails. Chaos became order under his eyes. In two well-formed lines, their courses now slightly divergent, his own and Onslow's divisions stood in towards the Dutch fleet.

'Mynheer de Winter's flagship is fifth in line,' he said to Fairfax. 'Pass through the line astern of her, then bring-to on her starboard side. Mr. Cleland, I want the larboard guns warned that they may be in action first.'

Cleland sprang down the ladder and hurried along the deck from gun to gun. Every one of the hundreds of figures down there was tense and ready; the guncrews stripped to the waist, the powder-boys waiting with their buckets, the two seamen at the ammunition hoist motionless with their hands on the tackle. Major Trollope's order (to Duncan it sounded exactly like the bark of a Scotch collie dog) was echoed by Lieutenant Chambers on the quarterdeck and the marines there went through their clockwork drill of loading and ramming.

The Dutch ships looked enormous now and grew larger every second. A watery gleam of sunshine touched the great yellow side of their flagship and struck transient colour in reflection from the grey waves under her flank. Even with the wind against the sound, the thin blare of a trumpet on her deck came to his ears. Shifting his glance, he saw Midshipman Stewart's white face screwed up tightly; the boy was standing with one hand on the signal locker and his eyes fixed on the Admiral. Yes – there was one last signal to be made.

'Make "Close action", Mr. Stewart. Number Five with the red pendant over. And leave it flying.'

'Starboard,' said Fairfax to the helmsman. 'Steady as you go.'

*Venerable* came slowly round a point and brought the wind right astern, heading straight for the enemy line. Behind her the other six ships of his Division did the same. *Monarch*, a cable's length away to starboard, was closing in fast – it looked as though Onslow would be first through the line. Ten minutes. Nine. . . .

'You can see the land, sir,' said Fairfax, coming up beside him.

It was dark and clear, that low bar on the horizon seen through the gap astern of the Dutch flagship. If there was anyone clinging to the steeple he could see sticking up they'd have a fine view of the coming battle.

'Mr. Porteous,' he said, 'can you name the village ashore yonder?'

'It's Kampenduin on their maps, sir,' said Porteous. 'On our charts it's Camperdown.'

# EIGHT

## I

In the years after the Battle of Camperdown Adam Duncan was to read and hear much criticism of his tactics on the fateful day of October 12th, 1797. Chief among the adverse critics was Earl St. Vincent, who declared that the action was 'fought pell-mell, without plan or system'. Duncan was able to smile at this comment from a great sea officer, knowing that St. Vincent was at that time penning a counterblast to John Clerk of Eldin in which he condemned the *Essay on Naval Tactics* as 'frippery and gimcrack'; and he could smile in a different fashion when he received a letter from Nelson a year after Camperdown, telling him how the one-armed Rear-Admiral had – as he put it – 'profited by Admiral Duncan's example' at the Battle of the Nile. The only criticism of Duncan from his own Fleet was made before the battle. Captain Inglis of *Belliqueux*, that irascible Scot, finding himself much puzzled by the Admiral's signals, hurled the signal-book to the deck with a roar of 'Damn old Adam and damn his bloody signals! Up with the hellum and gang into the middle o't!' Which, considering the last-minute countermanding of the order to form line, was perhaps excusable. Hotham of *Adamant* voiced the unanimous opinion of the captains when he wrote afterwards, 'had the Admiral done anything else but what he did, the day would not have been so decided'.

In the tense minutes before action Admiral Duncan had no doubts about the rightness of his decision. Erect, head flung back and hands behind back, he stood watching the narrowing strait of grey-green water between *Venerable* and her objective – watching, too, the closing gap between the Dutch flagship and a big black-sided ship, next astern in the enemy line, that carried a Rear-Admiral's flag. It would be touch-and-go if *Venerable* tried to get through that gap.

'Sir – they're drifting fast to leeward,' Porteous was saying urgently. 'It's likely we'll run aground—'

'Mr. Porteous, I'll fight 'em on land if that happens.'

Duncan took a long stride forward and snapped his orders. 'Quartermaster, starboard your helm. Steady— Mr. Cleland! Stand by the larboard broadside. Fire as your guns bear.'

As he spoke, a thunder of firing sounded from the Dutch rear. Onslow was into them, then. *Venerable*'s bowsprit swung to starboard as the helm was put over, pointing now just astern of the big black ship that had intervened between her and her first target. All her fore-and-aft sails flapped as the wind came over her starboard quarter. From the corner of his eye Duncan saw *Triumph*, who had been his next astern, taking a wider course to starboard; on the larboard beam *Ardent* was diverging in the other direction. All this must be happening very quickly, for the British ships were rushing forward with no diminution of sail except a double reef in the topsails, yet it seemed to Duncan that the two fleets, one presenting a wall to the battering-rams of the other, drew together with extraordinary slowness.

Suddenly there was nothing ahead of *Venerable* but open water: the gap in the line. Something hummed through the air overhead and a second later the noise was repeated *fortissimo*, followed by the multiple reports of musketry from the ships on either side of the gap. The flagship's for'ard guns opened fire with a stunning concussion, initiating the running broadside that poured into the stern of the black-painted ship as they flew past. Her carved timbers and high poop came sliding towards the quarterdeck and he saw big gilded letters above the stern windows: S, T, A – *Staten Generaal*. She was so close that he could have flung a stone into the great ragged hole that appeared as if by magic where two of the stern windows had been, and he could clearly see an officer pushing through the musketeers at the taffrail to level a pistol at him. The row of marines by the larboard rail in front of him fired their volley and officer and musketeers vanished from above the taffrail as if they had all been jerked back by strings. Then they were through the gap.

The following wind had blown the powder smoke away for'ard, so that he could see at once the execution done by *Venerable*'s upper deck guns. The *Staten Generaal* had lost most of her lower spars and her mizzen-mast was tilted at a drunken angle. No doubt that raking broadside had swept her deck, though he could see little of the damage there. But rudder or steering ropes had been put out of action, for she was falling off the wind, swinging round to point to the shore. Even now she was gathering way parallel to his own course, perversely interposing still between *Venerable* and the yellow flagship. To hold on until he could cross her bows would take him too far to leeward.

On either hand, now, the cannonade was increasing in noise and frequency as others of his ships came into action. It did not need Porteous's frenzied yell above the noise to tell him what he must do. Fairfax was looking anxiously at him, obviously waiting for the word. But Duncan's direct orders could save vital seconds.

'Hands to the braces! Hard a-larboard!'

*Venerable* heeled frighteningly as she was given full helm at racing speed. Duncan felt in his own body the tremendous strain on shrouds and rigging as her great masts tilted farther and farther over to starboard, and remembered with a qualm her aged timbers and the incomplete refit at Yarmouth. Fairfax down on deck was yelling through his speaking-trumpet at the hands who hauled on the braces to bring the yards round for a new course. The bowsprit was pointing straight at the black side of the *Staten Generaal* a hundred yards away and *Venerable*'s way was carrying her forward as if she intended to ram the Dutch ship amidships. With agonizing slowness now (as it seemed) the bows crept round to larboard. It was going to be a close-run thing. He made himself look away from the high black poop towering every moment higher ahead and observe the preparations on deck – the guns of the larboard broadside being run out again after reloading, Douglas dashing along the starboard guns to assure himself that each was ready.

'Starboard broadside! Fire as your guns bear!'

The dull glint of yellow ahead had drawn his eye like a magnet – De Winter's flagship was in full view. They were going to clear *Staten Generaal*'s stern by a few yards.

'Meet her!' Fairfax was shouting at the helmsman. 'Steady, now! Keep her—'

The roar of *Venerable*'s for'ard guns drowned the rest. For the second time, and at short range, she raked *Staten Generaal* from the stern. As far as Duncan could tell there was no reply. The black ship might well be out of the fight;

but he had eyes only for the huge yellow ship he was overhauling.

Fairfax came up to him as the after cannon ceased firing.

'One seaman dead, sir,' he reported. 'Three wounded. That broadside of theirs holed us twice, up in the bows. One's near the waterline.'

The Admiral narrowly avoided gaping at his Flag Captain like a halfwit. Just in time he recalled that the *Staten Generaal* had loosed a ragged broadside as *Venerable* was doubling on her track; he had been so concerned with the risk of collision that he had barely noticed it.

'Very good, Captain,' he said briefly. 'I want her stripped to tops'ls when I give the word. That'll be just before we engage the flagship yonder.'

'Aye aye, sir. Mr. Cleland's made out her name – *Vrijheid*. Means "Freedom", I understand.'

'Liberty, if the Dutch have adopted the Jacobin cant,' Duncan nodded, his grey eyes twinkling. 'Since we are fighting for freedom there must be a difference, would you not say?'

A great burst of firing ahead joined the now continuous thunder of the cannonade at the rear of the line. Peering for'ard beneath the giant screen of the mainsail they could see, beyond the yellow flagship, the dark shape of one ship and then another gliding across to starboard. In the drifting smoke of their broadsides they were not to be identified, but it was enough to know that they were through the Dutch line. For the Admiral it meant the end – for a time at least – of his greater responsibility; it was most unlikely that he would be able to exercise any control of tactics or strategy from this time forward until the issue was decided. Like any captain of a ship-of-the-line, he had merely to fight.

'We're coming up hand over fist,' Fairfax said 'Broadsides, sir?'

'Yes. Not until all guns bear. After the first broadside, independent firing. Please to pass that order to the deck officers, Captain.'

'Aye aye, sir.'

Fairfax moved away to speak to Cleland, who had come up the quarterdeck ladder. Duncan walked to the corner of the rail on the larboard side, the marines there making room for him as he approached. With his hands grasping the salt-sticky wood of the rail he stood immobile, his gaze on the *Vrijheid. Venerable* was coming up fast on the Dutch ship's starboard quarter; in five minutes he would be at death-grips with De Winter's flagship.

A rain-laden gust blew sharply across, gone almost as soon as it came. Perhaps it was the sting of the rain on Adam Duncan's cheek that initiated a curious illusion, as transient as the gust.

He was still an Admiral on his quarterdeck, but simultaneously he was looking down on himself from above – looking down on the whole battle line as a high-flying gull might view it, yet able to see with a new and piercing clarity the men on the decks, their expressions and their very thoughts. The ships were oddly shaped wooden boxes packed with the souls of men. A million lifetimes of human thought and toil had gone to make them what they were: the perfection of destructive power, their sole purpose the ending of other men's lives and the frustration of other men's plans. He saw the forest of great oaks that had been felled to build them, the mines whence had come the ores for making the cannon and their iron balls; the labour of twenty thousand women in childbirth, to bear sons who would kill and be killed in their prime; the ingenuity and learning of scholars since time began, to contrive instruments by whose use the two collections of wooden boxes could find each other in the waste of oceans and destroy all that had been built or nurtured. He saw (in that unnerving vision) how all men were right and all men wrong. For if those hundred-and-eighty mutineers imprisoned in the hulks were misguided children who had tried to do what they thought was right, so too were the Jacobins who strove to give Liberty and Equality to mankind. Where was Providence in this? Was it the implacable Decree that men should slaughter and disembowel each other in their struggle towards the light?

He was down there on the deck with Cleland now – Cleland with his gay smile and his shining eyes, winning answering grins from the guncrews as he passed with his springy stride. There was no more thought of struggling for an ideal in Cleland than there was in the brawny gunners whose spirits he was linking with his own. They were in the grip of a trained and disciplined savagery; they were what the Navy – and Adam Duncan – had made them. They would toil and suffer, endure and die, without complaint because they had been taught that this was their duty, and also because (he saw this suddenly) the ordeal was their opportunity to prove themselves of different mettle from the beasts that perish. He seemed to dwell for a moment of time in the mind of Frowde, the mutinous seaman whom he had so nearly spitted on his sword. Frowde's spirit was being transmuted by the imminence of death into something worthy to stand in company with the spirits of saints and martyrs, for the fear of death had been sloughed with the rags of lust and petty vice that had clothed it. With Frowde's shipmates it was the same: the 'brute beasts' of Earl Spencer's phrase had become heroes by this magic of the uplifted spirit. And yet their purpose was to kill. It was insane – illogical – wrong, that men could approach so near to God by a means that had nothing at all of God in it. He felt the crumbling of his faith, saw the path of Duty ending in a quagmire. The clouds darkened round him and he seemed falling through them towards a cluster of ships infinitely small on the face of great waters. . . .

'Sir!'

Fairfax's voice was both urgent and anxious. The Admiral started, as from an evil dream, and saw reality demanding his instant attention. *Venerable* had drawn to within half a cable of the Dutch flagship.

'Take in sail, Captain!'

The order sprang from his lips at once. He was conscious of something fading swiftly from his mind, some vanishing reflection that had been damnably disturbing. What it had been he could not remember, but it had left him with an odd sense of relief at finding himself able to think again as an Admiral should. Day-dreaming, woolgathering at such a moment! It was a senile failing, and there was nothing senile about him now. His spirit was again the spirit of his ship and of the men who were that ship – the topmen working aloft to strip her for the fight, the gunners eagerly poised and waiting on her decks.

*Venerable*'s way fell off as her sail area was reduced. Very close now, the high yellow poop of De Winter's flagship grew slowly larger; the rows of gunports, each with its threatening muzzle just protruding, extended as the British ship came up and widened his angle of view. Beyond her was a cloud of smoke flecked with orange lightnings, in which he could see the black stern of *Ardent*. The continuous uproar of *Ardent*'s action drowned the rattle of musketry from *Vrijheid*'s after rail, and Duncan's first intimation that he was under fire came when his hat was twitched from his head and sent flying across the quarterdeck. Roscoe, the senior midshipman, picked it up and handed it to him. Roscoe's eyes, big as saucers, were fixed on the ragged hole made by the musketball in the crown. The Admiral remembered how the headband had chafed his forehead and returned the hat to the midshipman.

'Being subject to colds in the head, Mr. Roscoe,' he said gravely, 'I had rather not wear this. Pray tuck it under the netting on the taffrail.'

For the life of him he could not repress the senseless elation that bubbled up in him, and the jest, feeble though it was, was the expression of it. *Venerable*'s bowsprit was overlapping *Vrijheid*'s stern.

'Fire!' screeched Chambers, and the quarterdeck detachment of marines fired their volley.

The for'ard guns were bearing now. The gunners, with musket-balls from the Dutchman's tops humming about them, must be itching to loose off in reply – one seaman, he saw, was motionless on the deck behind his gun with blood all over his face. Fairfax's anxious shout of 'hold your fire!' showed that the same thought had occurred to him. A puff of smoke spurted from *Vrijheid*'s aftermost gunport and the ball screamed low across the quarterdeck. Looking round quickly to see if anyone was hit, Duncan saw Midshipman Stewart, a few paces from him, bent almost double with his hand clasped over his hat. He tapped the boy on the shoulder.

'Hold your head up, Mr. Stewart. You might put it in the way of the next ball like that.'

Evidently that one gun had fired without orders, for the Dutch flagship's broadside was as silent as *Venerable*'s while the latter advanced slowly board-and-board with her. The infernal racket of the musketry from both ships was scarcely audible against the din of continuous firing from the line ahead and astern; yet to Duncan it seemed that the two flagships drew together in silence, so tense were those final moments. Then it came, with unlooked-for violence.

The two broadsides roared out simultaneously. The discharge of seventy-two cannon in unison seemed to split the sky asunder and drive a man's eardrums into his head.

*Venerable*, rocking with the concussion of her own broadside, was flung farther over by the impact of the well-aimed balls from *Vrijheid*. The leap and shudder of her sent the Admiral pitching to the deck, but he had scrambled to his feet before Fairfax could help him up.

'Tops'l braces, Captain – keep her on the wind!'

He was unaware that he was shouting; to his deafened ears his voice sounded thin and far away. No matter how fierce the fighting, *Venerable*'s greatest danger lay in the shoal water under her lee. At all costs she must be kept from drifting to starboard.

## II

From that moment onward Duncan had to judge the progress of the fight from a series of disjointed impressions – glimpses instantly blotted out by drifting smoke, sounds heard in a brief interval of the cannonade, reports brought to him by breathless officers. With *Vrijheid* to windward of him, the acrid powder-smoke from her guns as well as from the larboard guns of his own ship blew across *Venerable*'s decks in billowing clouds that cleared only occasionally to show him what was happening amidships and for'ard. And there was no cessation in the deafening thunder.

After that first simultaneous exchange of broadsides, his concern had been to learn the comparative rates of fire of the Dutch and British gunners. If he had anxiety on that count it was quickly set at rest. *Venerable*'s second broadside roared out a second before the Dutch flagship's reply came. It was a ragged broadside, but the fact that the detonations sounded so closely together meant that the guncrews were almost equally efficient; they were firing independently now, each gun discharging its ball as fast as the crew could reload. Sponge, load, ram, run out, and fire – the gun drill that had occupied so many hours during the long months of the Texel blockade was bearing fruit now. Through ragged gaps in the smoke he could catch sight, now and then, of the half-naked men working like demons. As near as he could estimate, they were firing three shots to the Dutchman's two.

'We're making leeway, sir!' Porteous said loudly in his ear.

A long splinter torn from the quarterdeck rail whizzed

close to his face as he spoke, but he did not flinch or change his worried expression. Porteous, Duncan realized suddenly, was much more afraid of shoal water than of death or wounds. He nodded and turned, but *Venerable* was bringing her bows nearer the wind already; Fairfax had gone to stand beside the helm and the necessary order had been given. As well as he could for the smoke, Duncan watched the yellow flank of the Dutch flagship. She, too, was bearing up a little, keeping her distance. The last thing De Winter would want was to give his adversary the chance of boarding. St. Vincent – and earlier seafights too – had taught the world that British seamen swarming aboard cutlass in hand were irresistible.

De Winter would rely on his gunnery. And his guns, if they were rather less expertly handled than the British, were doing execution. The Admiral saw that six feet of the quarterdeck rail had gone leaving a ragged gap; presumably the shot that had sent the splinter close to the Pilot had done that. But the real damage to his ship was invisible from the quarterdeck. With the wind and waves on their beams, both ships were rolling slightly as they forged slowly ahead side by side in their cocoon of smoke, and the Dutch gunners were firing on the down-roll. As if they knew the weakness of *Venerable*'s aged timbers, they were pounding her sides with nearly every shot. The chain-pump was already working its hardest to keep down the water in her leaky hold and a couple of sizeable holes on the waterline could mean—

'Starboard beam, sir – enemy vessel!'

Paterson had dashed across from the lee rail to get his attention. He was pointing urgently to the dun smoke-clouds that drifted away to leeward, and Duncan saw the black side of a ship come pushing through them a scant two hundred yards away. He recognized her by her mizzen-mast, which leaned drunkenly against the main rigging; the *Staten Generaal* was entering the fight again. The black side sprouted a double row of yellow flames as he looked, and before the smoke of her broadside blew clear *Venerable*'s starboard guns had roared a reply. Overhead there was a groan and a crack, and a fifteen-foot spar – half the shattered spanker-yard – crashed into the *sauve-tête* netting with a tangle of blocks and cordage.

The Admiral, frowning, passed a big hand across his

chin. Attacked on both flanks, *Venerable* was twice as likely to founder; he knew only too well the state of her planking on the waterline. The dreadful thought of his aged ship sinking with all her guns still in action had barely crossed his mind when the deck beneath him leaped and shuddered as to a multiple hammer-blow. Those shots had come from astern. He swung round to see a Dutch two-decker, like the yellow wraith of a ship in the smoke-haze, turning slowly to the wind after firing. Mr. Brown, the second pilot, was facing him and waving an arm at this new menace, unnecessarily calling his attention to it. Brown's mouth was open to speak when it was suddenly ripped into a horrid red gash. He fell writhing and screaming to the deck, his jaw broken by the musket-shot. The two seamen who came running up the ladder at Roscoe's hail lifted Brown to take him below; their bare arms, Duncan noted, were crimsoned to the elbows.

But he could think only of *Venerable*'s case, beset as she was three to one. And in the well-nigh intolerable din of the firing it was difficult, now, to think at all. All *Venerable*'s guns were firing, and with the continuous pounding from *Vrijheid*'s starboard guns and the more distant thunder from *Staten Generaal* there was no pause in the stunning, stultifying uproar. To steady himself he looked at his watch: a quarter to two. It seemed incredible that an hour had passed since he had passed through the enemy line.

A shrill sound of cheering cut through the deeper roaring of the guns. To get to the larboard rail he had to step over the body of a marine; the man's coat gleamed like a breastplate, dark and shiny with blood. He looked up from it to see the Dutch flagship's main topmast plunging down with the torn sail streaming from it like the tailing of a kite. It struck *Vrijheid*'s rail and its splintered end flailed round, knocking overboard three or four men, before it dropped to dangle by its cordage against the ship's side. The smoke from the discharge of his after guns blotted out the sight, and a second later the planking of the quarterdeck three paces from him sprang up in huge white splinters as though some horned monster were ripping it from beneath. The shot that did that had come from astern again. Where were the ships of his division that should be engaging that yellow ship in his rear? *Powerful* should be thereabouts, and Drury was not the man to hold aloof from a fight.

Another burst of cheering made him peer eagerly into the pall of smoke to leeward, and through a momentary rift he caught sight of a ship's poop, almost hidden in a drapery of torn sails and shattered spars, gliding away; *Staten Generaal*'s short attack had been beaten off and it appeared unlikely that she would return. Nor was there any more of that unnerving fire from the yellow ship astern of him. (He learned later that she was the *Wassenaer*, 64, and that *Powerful* had battered her into surrender ten minutes after her last raking shots at the flagship.) But the fury of firing between his own ship and De Winter's seemed to increase rather than diminish. The British gunners tended to aim high, largely because of *Venerable*'s slight list to starboard under the pressure of the northerly wind, and every time he glimpsed *Vrijheid*'s masts and spars there was fresh damage to be seen. Her mizzen-mast appeared to have been almost severed near its base and was kept from falling only by a cat's-cradle of tangled cordage; her mainyard was gone, the main topsail above it shredded into long rags of canvas that flapped in the wind. There was a little comfort in this to set against the endless crashing of her shot into *Venerable*'s wounded sides.

A hand touched his arm. The Second Lieutenant stood at his side, shouting to make himself heard above the guns.

'Mr. Cleland's compliments, sir – Mr. Clay's wounded – ball carried off his arm – would suggest Mr. Roscoe—'

Douglas's hat was gone and his white waistcoat was filthy with powder stains. His face was blackened too, except where the blood from a long gash on his cheek had run down it to soak into his stock.

'Very good, Mr. Douglas,' Duncan roared back. 'Mr. Roscoe! Take charge of the after guns.'

'One for'ard gun dismounted, sir.' Douglas was continuing his report. 'Seven dead, thirty wounded, so far. Most of the larboard rail's gone and the spritsail's carried away. And we've no boats left, sir – cutter and longboat went to matchwood ten minutes ago.'

'Very good,' said Duncan again; he was momentarily conscious of the ineptness of the words. 'Carry on, Mr. Douglas.'

Douglas leaped down into the swirling smoke as if he was eager to go. It had been on the tip of Duncan's tongue to ask him if *Venerable* had been holed below the waterline for'ard, but Douglas could hardly be expected to know that. He called to Paterson to go below and examine the water-level in the hold.

He had thought he was becoming accustomed to the inferno of noise, but that phase seemed to be passing. The unremitting bellow of the guns was hammering at his mind, beating it into a dull misery of endurance, and he had to exercise a continuous effort of will to keep his senses on the alert. The conviction that it could not last much longer grew in him as the minutes passed. No human being, no thing made of human hands, could stand the strain. For ninety minutes now the men had been slaving at the guns; for ninety minutes the wooden sides of both ships had been battered by cannonballs. Dutch or English, *Vrijheid* or *Venerable* – the moment of collapse must come for the one or the other.

The firing from the Dutchman's tops had ceased. Her maintop had been shattered by gunfire and the musketeers in the mizzen-top must have been flung to their deaths when the mast was severed. But there was still continuous shooting from her poop, to which his marines – only five of them were still at the rail, he saw – were replying. Here came Paterson up the ladder, his lean face grim.

'Upwards of a fathom in the hold, sir, and rising fast,' was his shouted report. 'Mr. Cleland's got a party plugging the shot-holes nearest the waterline, but she's been holed at least thirty times 'tween wind and water. I've started both hand-pumps as well as the chain—'

He staggered back and fell on one knee, clutching at his thigh. Blood welled out between his fingers. At Duncan's sharp order one of the marines laid down his musket and took hold of Paterson's shoulders while the Pilot took his legs. Porteous had a bullet-score across his scalp and the trickle of blood into his eyes set him swearing as they started to carry Paterson down the ladder.

'Look, sir! Look! Look!'

It was Midshipman Stewart, positively tugging at the Admiral's coat as he screeched excitedly. The boy's eyes were unnaturally bright and his thin cheeks flushed, as if he had the fever. Duncan looked where he pointed.

*Vrijheid* could be seen more clearly, for nearly all her guns for'ard of the mainmast had ceased to fire. And the mainmast was going – leaning slowly, slowly over to starboard. Then it stopped, its fall checked by the larboard shrouds. She was disabled, at any rate, for he saw now that her foremast had gone as well. She must strike – surely she would strike! But half-a-dozen of her after guns were blazing still, with (it seemed) greater fury than ever. With no sail drawing, *Vrijheid* was almost stopped, and *Venerable* was fore-reaching on her. He heard Fairfax yelling for hands to man the braces, to back the topsails. But already the quarterdeck of the British ship had drawn level with those furious guns. He heard the scream of the balls and saw a broad white groove open in the base of the mizzenmast. The few marines still at the rail were suddenly hurled clear across the deck with the ruins of the rail on top of them. Chambers dropped to the deck beside him with a two foot splinter sticking out of his side like a spear, and as he bent over the marine captain another body – Stewart's – fell across Chambers. Stewart was unconscious from a head wound. That looked superficial, but blood was pulsing from his torn left sleeve in a dark stream. His left hand was gone.

The Admiral straightened up to glance round him. The quarterdeck was a chaos, a litter of torn wood and bodies that writhed or lay still; he was the only man alive and unhurt. And the boy must be got to the surgeon. He picked him up in his arms and started down the ladder.

'I can't hold her on course, sir!' Fairfax yelled from beside the helm as he passed; there were two corpses, one headless, at the Flag Captain's feet. 'Steering-rope's parted – we're reeving a new rope.'

Duncan nodded at him without halting. There were tracks and rivulets of blood across the deck. Two hands passed him at a trot, carrying a man whose naked chest was a mangled red pulp. He peered this way and that into the swirling smoke, looking for seamen who could carry Stewart to the cockpit, but there were no unoccupied men to be seen. Except dead men. Dead men lay like bundles or heaps of red rags in the scuppers between the guns, while the gunners wrought like demons in the stygian vapours above them. At one gun, he saw, a woman with her skirts kilted to the thigh was hauling on the tackles beside her man; a blatant contravention of orders, but he had no time for that now. As he strode round a pile of debris that included the remains of the cutter he came upon portions of another body – a seaman, literally torn in two by a ball. Beyond it was the midships hatchway. The stench from below drove up at him in a nauseous blast as he carried Stewart down the ladder, and the sight that met his eyes at the bottom made him halt with one foot still on the lowest step.

Blood and the stink of blood was everywhere. Blood swilled on the decks where wounded and mutilated seamen lay like beasts maimed before slaughtering, waiting their turn on the blood-soaked benches where, by the smoky light of two hanging lanterns, the bare-armed surgeon and his mates wielded knife and saw. The noise was deafening, rising above the crash of shot and the reverberant thunder of the cannonade – groans and shrieks and wails, prayers and defiant snatches of song. The sights and sounds and smells sent the Admiral back up the ladder as fast as he had come down it. It was physically impossible for him to leave Stewart there.

Fortune aided him. A second after he emerged on deck again he perceived his Secretary. Mr. Burnet was stepping gingerly through the smoke-wreaths, moving his round spectacled head from side to side, like a tortoise.

'I was seeking you, sir,' he said portentously as soon as he caught sight of the Admiral. 'A shot having penetrated your cabin, it is no longer—'

'Take him.' Duncan thrust the midshipman's slight figure into Burnet's arms. 'Your cabin, and quickly. Apply a tourniquet – left arm. You know how to do that?'

'I – ah – yes, sir,' stammered the Secretary, staggering beneath the unexpected burden. 'There are, I believe, bandages—'

Duncan left him and went with long strides towards the quarterdeck ladder. Something was happening. The ship's motion had changed – and surely the fire of the guns was slackening? A whistle shrilled and Fairfax's voice cut clearly through the lessened tumult.

'Cease fire! – D'ye hear, there? Cease fire!'

The First Lieutenant came rushing past him, spun on his heel as he saw it was the Admiral.

'*Vrijheid*'s struck, sir!' Cleland's teeth gleamed dazzling white in his blackened face. 'She's struck – and so has another Dutchman ahead of us. I saw the colours come down. By God, sir, I believe we've beat 'em!'

Duncan stood quite motionless for a moment, at the foot of the quarterdeck ladder. There was still plenty of noise – some cannon-fire distantly astern, the clanking of the pumps, the faint but heartrending chorus of the wounded – but after the uproar of his duel with De Winter it seemed a heavenly silence. He turned to look across the larboard rail, where the exhausted gunners had collapsed by their guns to lie as limply as their dead mates. *Vrijheid*, with all her masts gone, was a lifeless hulk – and her torn yellow flank was now twice as far from *Venerable* as it had been before he had left the quarterdeck. It was moving farther away as he looked.

Fairfax, approaching across the littered deck, answered the Admiral's frown before he could voice his question.

'She won't bear up, sir. She's answering helm, though, and we can wear and come up on the starboard tack to *Vrijheid*.'

'Very good, Captain. But we must take possession. Send a boat away, if you please, and request Admiral De Winter—' Duncan checked himself; there was no boat to send away. 'Make that manœuvre as fast as you can, Captain,' he amended the order. 'And hail the first of our ships you may see to send a boat to *Vrijheid*. Mr. Cleland, keep the men standing to their guns.'

He had time to think of Stewart now. Stewart was only thirteen, with his life before him if Burnet didn't bungle that tourniquet. Henrietta had taught him about arteries and pressure, and it might be as well—

The Admiral turned and strode towards Burnet's cabin.

## III

They had news of the battle from *Director* fifteen minutes later. Captain William Bligh brought his 64-gun ship within hail of *Venerable* as she was wearing round half-a-mile from the Dutch flagship, having come up from the rear of the line where six of the enemy had struck to their opponents. In the van the firing had ceased altogether and one Dutch 64 was on fire; now that the gloomy sea and sky were clearly visible again, it could be seen that two at least of the leading Dutch ships had struck. There was no doubt in Duncan's mind that his Fleet had won an overwhelming victory, though it was much later before the full tale – eleven ships of the line and three Dutch admirals taken – was told; later still when the sheaves of reports revealed the numbers of the dead, 228 Englishmen and 330 Dutch men.

Captain Bligh was ordered to send a boat to *Vrijheid* and bring Admiral De Winter on board. Duncan, as happy in the knowledge that Midshipman Stewart would live as in the destruction of the Batavian Fleet, had some minutes in which to prepare for De Winter's reception on board. He retrieved his uncomfortable hat from the hammock netting, where it had miraculously survived with no damage additional to the bullet-hole. He changed his white breeches (they were stained with Stewart's blood) for a clean pair laid out for him by Menzies. He rehearsed a series of neat phrases which should convey his genuine admiration for *Vrijheid*'s gallant and stubborn fight.

De Winter came slowly up over the side from *Director*'s boat. He was a tall man, nearly as tall as Duncan, with the calm features of a scholar and thinker. The British Admiral, hat in hand, received him at the foot of the quarter-deck ladder.

'Admiral Duncan,' said the Dutchman sadly, 'I am the first of my nation to do this.'

He held out his sword, hilt foremost. Duncan's stilted phrases fled from his mind. He took a step forward and held out his big fist.

'Put it by, sir, put it by,' he said, 'and give me your hand instead.'

# EPILOGUE

'He's late,' frowned the Secretary for War, shaking his watch and holding it to his ear.

'He will not come,' said the Prime Minister with finality; he replaced his own watch in his fob. 'Adam Duncan is not interested in us, Harry.'

They stood together in the bay window of the Royal Academy Club, looking down through the long curtains at the cobbles of Gerrard Street glistening in the rain. From the inner room behind them came the continuous murmur of men's voices, with a perceptible undertone of querulousness; dinner was to have been served at three and it was now five minutes past the hour.

'Baron Duncan of Lundie, first Viscount Camperdown,' Dundas muttered. 'Ten thousand in prize money, gold medals, gold swords, freedoms of three capital cities – it could go to a man's head, forbye he's an old man.'

Pitt pursed his thin lips. 'He was not definite with you he would come, I believe.'

'He mumbled some nonsense about a short voyage. Inferred it might prevent him reaching Gerrard Street if wind and tide were adverse.' Dundas pushed his fingers under his wig to scratch his head. 'Where would he go voyaging in London, unless it's the River? Would ye say, Billy, he's given us the go-by?'

'I think it certain.'

'But – Gad's me life! Here's half the Cabinet and the Prince to dine with him, not to mention you and me—'

'Whatever his reason,' Pitt interrupted, 'it impresses Lord Duncan more strongly than your efforts to recruit him to the Tory cause, sir. I advise you to abandon them.'

'But he's the most popular man in England,' Dundas protested.

'And probably the most honest. As a politician, I fancy, your noble and venerable nephew would scarcely—'

'*Holà,* gentlemen! Are we to dine or are we not?'

A fat man in a salmon-pink coat stood in the doorway eyeing them owlishly, a frown on his pouchy face. The

Prime Minister and the Secretary turned towards him as one man.

'Immediately, sir, immediately,' said Dundas hastily. 'If your Royal Highness will precede us—'

The Prince nodded, swung round on his high red heels, and vanished into the inner room again. The two Ministers followed.

'We'll drink Adam's health, none the less,' Dundas murmured. 'When all's said, he saved the Government.'

'He saved England,' said Pitt. 'But it would be interesting,' he added reflectively as they passed through the doorway, 'to know where he is at this moment.'

At that moment Adam Duncan, first Viscount Camperdown, was sitting in the sternsheets of a wherry pulling out from the dockyard steps at Chatham. Rain drove across the dingy waters of the Medway, soaking his boat-cloak and hiding all his surroundings except the grim black prison-ships towards which the boat was heading, but Duncan's face was serene and his grey eyes happy. Beneath the boat-cloak, clutched in one big hand, he held a precious document signed by the King himself. It was a Free Pardon and Order of Release for a hundred and eighty of his erring children.

ADMIRAL OF ENGLAND

Clowdisley Shovell was one of our great sea officers during the most exciting period in British history, when the ferment of revolution was threatening the power of the Stuart kings.

*Admiral of England* is the grippingly authentic novel of that supreme fighting seaman and the swash-buckling violence of his battles. It follows Shovell through daring exploits against Mediterranean pirates and bloody conflict with the French fleet to the final tragic climax of his career.

Here is a story of action on the high seas, guaranteed to delight the legions of readers who thrill to superb maritime adventure.